"COME HERE!"

"Why should I?"

"Because you're my wife!" Swiftly, he crossed the intervening space and grasped her tightly, his fingers digging into her arm. "Don't move away from me!"

Although she tried to pull back, his hold was too strong. "Let me go!"

"No! You're my wife. I can do practically anything I want." His jaws clenched.

"This is the twentieth century. . . . I have rights!"

"Oh, really," he drawled menacingly. "So do I." He ran his hands across the silky fabric covering her shoulders and neck. His eyes flickered over her. "Admit you are ready and willing!"

LEIGH RICHARDS
is an American author whose vivid prose brings to life her fascinating characters and ever-changing landscapes. Her intriguing plots will continue to surprise and delight her many readers.

Dear Reader:

Silhouette Romances is an exciting new publishing venture. We will be presenting the very finest writers of contemporary romantic fiction as well as outstanding new talent in this field. It is our hope that our stories, our heroes and our heroines will give you, the reader, all you want from romantic fiction.

Also, *you* play an important part in our future plans for Silhouette Romances. We welcome any suggestions or comments on our books and I invite you to write to us at the address below.

So, enjoy this book and all the wonderful romances from Silhouette. They're for *you!*

Karen Solem
Editor-in-Chief
Silhouette Books
P. O. Box 769
New York, N.Y. 10019

LEIGH RICHARDS
Spring Fires

Silhouette Romance

Published by Silhouette Books New York

SILHOUETTE BOOKS, a Simon & Schuster Division of
GULF & WESTERN CORPORATION
1230 Avenue of the Americas, New York, N.Y 10020

SILHOUETTE BOOKS, a Simon & Schuster division of
GULF & WESTERN CORPORATION
1230 Avenue of the Americas, New York, N.Y. 10020

Copyright © 1980 by Leigh Richards

Distributed by Pocket Books

ISBN: 0-671-57021-8

First Silhouette printing July, 1980

10 9 8 7 6 5 4 3 2 1

Printed in the U.S.A.

To All My Friends Who Helped Me

Chapter One

Stacy Davidson gazed out across the green acres of grazing land to the billowing black clouds of smoke which the unrelenting winds had carried across miles of the eastern horizon where the sun was attempting to proclaim the beginning of another day. The newly drilled oil well had blown out and the ensuing fire had been burning out of control for thirty-six hours. Her father, Bob Davidson, was out at the site directing his roughnecks as they valiantly fought to control the fire and save their equipment. Too restless to nap during a break, Stacy paced the ground in front of the trailer. Her normally vibrant features were masked by stress and exhaustion. Drooping lids hid her dark brown eyes and violet circles pronounced a lack of sleep.

Her eyes shifted away from the fire to the empty road which came from the north. Stacy strained to catch the first glimpse of whirling dust heralding the arrival of the

Jeep℠. Her father's assistant, Paul Elmwood, had driven to the nearest air field to meet the private plane of Drew Pitman, the famous oil-well fire-fighter. In such emergencies, most drilling companies contracted his unique skills and courage to evaluate and extinguish the blazing hellfires. With his highly trained fearless crews, Drew had handled fires where standard techniques had failed at drilling sites scattered throughout the southwestern United States and Gulf of Mexico.

Finally, Stacy's vigil was rewarded as small clouds of dust appeared on the horizon. She crossed her fingers and prayed that this was the expected arrival. Drew Pitman had waited until dawn to fly in from Houston.

Startled out of her contemplations, Stacy turned as she heard the familiar sound of a pickup coming from the direction of the oil rig. Her puzzled expression was replaced by a look of concern as her father climbed down from the truck to join her. The effects of long hours of back-breaking work were all too apparent. His usual brisk pace was gone, his broad shoulders were bent, and his greying hair completed an image of a tired old man; he was only fifty-eight years old.

She fixed an encouraging smile on her face and pointed to a Jeep℠ rapidly tearing up the miles. "That should be them," she guessed.

"None too soon," said Bob tersely as he followed the Jeep℠ with his eyes.

Stacy firmly suppressed her desire to comfort him; this was neither the time nor the place. What her father needed, she thought wistfully, was sleep; but he could not relax until the crisis had passed. Instead, she watched the grimy Jeep℠, now recognizable by the bright red company insignia emblazoned on its side. Two men were seated in it.

Bob Davidson stood numbly until the Jeep℠ pulled

up. Then he walked over to the passenger side as the newcomer leapt out.

The tall stranger held out his powerful right hand to the older man. "Drew Pitman," he said confidently.

"Good to meet you, Drew. I'm Bob Davidson." His voice sounded brighter and he squared his shoulders as he shook the younger man's hand.

Stacy stood by, quietly listening as Drew Pitman thrust pleasantries aside and stated, "I must visit the site immediately. The weather forecast is bad, so we need to move fast."

"Fine," returned Bob. "We'll take my pickup and Paul can follow in the Jeep™. I'll fill you in on the casing and well head."

"Good. Let's go!"

Watching the men leave, Stacy was heartened by the positive reaction of her father to this "expert." Her eyes focused on Drew Pitman's retreating figure. His head topped Bob's six feet by several inches. He was a big man in a big job. Everything now depended on his skill and knowledge. She had assumed that he was much older since she had heard so many tales of his exploits, but he appeared to be in his early thirties. His features were set in ruggedly masculine lines; the firm planes of his cheeks and jaw were softened only slightly by thick, wavy, sun-streaked blond hair falling across his forehead and curling over the collar of his blue work shirt. His long legs easily carried him over the rough ground to the pickup. The movements of his hard muscular body conveyed an image of a champion athlete whose controlled looseness was tempered imperceptibly by the anticipation of meeting a worthy challenger.

A shuffling of feet to Stacy's left interrupted her thoughts. Turning, she saw Paul Elmwood waiting to

speak with her and could not avoid an instant comparison. Paul's mildly pleasant features and light brown
hair diminished his substance, while Drew's were
powerfully solid.

"Yes, Paul? Is there something you need?" Stacy was
irritated by the shortness of her voice.

Paul shifted his bulk from one foot to the other
before he answered, "How are you holding up?"

"Just fine. Probably better than most."

"That's good. You should take care of yourself." His
voice held a possessive note which startled her.

"Paul, until this crisis is over we all have to set aside
our personal needs."

"But a woman doesn't have as much stamina as a
man."

"Oh, really?" Her voice was cool, but her mind
seethed. Quickly she reminded herself that this was not
the time for a discussion of the capabilities of men
versus women.

Oblivious to her irritation, Paul said, "I'll be going."

"Okay. See you later." Stacy was relieved to see him
leave and did not wait until he had started the Jeep™
before she went back into the trailer.

She spent the next hour working steadily, putting
together a variety of thick meat sandwiches, pitchers of
iced tea, and pots of hot coffee. It took her several trips
to carry everything outside to the long utility table set
up for the men. Next she checked the supplies of food
and called in the delivery order to the grocery store in
the nearest town.

As Stacy hung up the phone, her ears picked up the
sound of engines; she hurried out with the pitcher of
iced tea and the coffeepot. After all of the men were
served, she headed back to her trailer for a break.

The trailer had been her home for the past several

weeks since the well had passed ten thousand feet. Usually the team put up in motels near the site. But due to the forty-mile distance, they had opted for travel trailers at a recreational vehicle camp five miles from the well. Stacy shared one with her father.

The quarters were cramped; the living area was filled with office equipment—a desk with a swivel chair and filing cabinets—and, for comfort, a small tweed sofa. To the left next to the kitchen were four vinyl-covered dinette chairs and a Formica™ table which could be folded down against the wall. The kitchen itself was compact, with a two-burner stove, stainless-steel sink, and a built-in refrigerator. Cabinets above the work counter held dishes and glassware while a small broom closet doubled as a pantry. Cartons of extra foodstuffs were set in the corner along with a large cooler filled with beer and ice.

Stacy was leaning back in one of the chairs with her feet propped up on the desk when the door opened. Her father entered first, followed by Drew Pitman, Paul bringing up the rear. Instantly the room was charged with energy. She hastily dropped her feet to the floor and stood up awaiting instructions.

Bob requested shortly, "Coffee."

Drew spared Stacy a penetrating glance before he dropped several papers on the desk. "Let's review this plan."

Bob and Paul huddled around the desk listening intently to Drew's authoritative recommendation.

Stacy went to the kitchen. She had held in reserve a Thermos™ of coffee which she swiftly poured out into thick white mugs. She added jars of creamer and sugar and spoons to a tray and carried it over to the men.

Drew raised his head as he heard the gentle rustling movements of Stacy's denim-clad legs. Stunned by the devastating effect of his midnight-blue eyes, she paused momentarily; but she quickly collected her jangled nerves to serve her father and Paul. As she held out the last mug to Drew, she was caught again by the spell of those eyes and found it impossible to control the slight tremor in her hand. She fervently hoped he would not notice, but she saw, in his derisive smile, understanding. She pointedly turned to her father. "Anything else?"

Drew answered for them all. "Not right now."

She glanced back as he lifted the corner of his mouth in a provocative smile that would liquidate the resistance of any red-blooded female.

I will not let him get to me, Stacy told herself firmly. *He is just an arrogant male, accomplished at practicing his masculine charms on every available woman.*

She stepped back from the desk, about to return to the kitchen, when Bob forestalled her retreat.

"Stacy, I haven't introduced you to Drew Pitman." He looked at Drew and smiled proudly. "This is my daughter, Stacy. She's my personal secretary as well as temporary cook for the crew."

Stacy hesitated and then answered with unconcealed formality, "I'm pleased to meet you, Mr. Pitman." She awkwardly extended a pale slender hand, which was immediately enveloped by firm fingers.

"Hello, Stacy. Too bad the men don't have enough time to appreciate such an attractive cook."

Her eyes dropped to conceal the sparks of resentment as she sensed an underlying censure in his comment.

Paul, not to be excluded any longer, pompously interjected, "Stacy is an amazing girl."

The blue eyes continued their sardonic appraisal. "I'm sure she is."

Stacy's expression was decidedly frosty as she ignored his quip and pivoted on her heel to walk back to the kitchen.

Her hands were busy but her mind burned with annoyance over Drew's condescending attitude. *What right does he have to judge me? I may work for my father, but I put in long, hard hours!* She tossed her hair back over her shoulder. *No* man *can do any better!*

Out of the corner of her eye, Stacy unobtrusively watched the subject of her anger. After the men had completed the final details for their attack on the fire, Drew moved decisively to the phone and dialed. "John, I want your crew on this one. How soon can you get here . . . ? Good." He listed the specific equipment he wanted and gave directions.

Drew replaced the receiver and leaned back in his chair to drink his coffee. He let his eyes wander over the walls of the room until they were arrested by Stacy's restless movements.

The hairs on the back of her neck tingled as she sensed someone watching. She glanced surreptitiously over her shoulder and caught Drew's watchful regard. Challenged by his stare, she continued to focus on him, attempting to return a disinterested look. It lasted until he slowly closed one eye in an exaggerated wink.

Oh, this is silly! she admonished herself, and she shrugged a shoulder derisively as she turned back to her task. What nerve! The insolent . . .

Stacy, distracted, clumsily fumbled with the lid she was replacing on the creamer jar. Everything slid through her fingers and she muttered an oath as it shattered on the linoleum. Quickly she stooped down to pick up the fragments, swearing softly as a sliver pierced her index finger, sending a shot of pain up her arm. Conscientiously, she dropped the shards into the trashcan before grabbing a paper towel to check the flow of blood.

The next instant Stacy felt strong fingers clamp around her wrist, lifting her injured hand.

"Just what have you done?" Drew bit out.

"I dropped a jar and was cleaning up the mess," returned Stacy pugnaciously.

"Without a broom?"

"I forgot."

"Oh, Lord, save me from impetuous females." Drew rolled his eyes dramatically and then trained his eyes on her. "Where is your first-aid kit?"

"In that cupboard above your head." But she added swiftly, "I'll take care of it myself."

"Like you took care of the jar? Hmmm . . . ? Just cooperate."

The penetrating tones did not pierce Bob's thoughtful silence, but Paul looked up questioningly. Stacy shook her head in answer to his unspoken concern.

Long, dextrous fingers gently probed the wound for more glass. Then Drew held her hand over the sink to thoroughly clean it with soap and water. After he applied medicated ointment, he wrapped it with a Band-aid.

"There, that should take care of it, but keep it dry."

"Yes, sir. Thank you, sir." Stacy could not suppress her sarcastic retort.

"Don't get cheeky with me, girl. You don't know what you're letting yourself in for," admonished Drew with a flick of his finger against her cheek to emphasize his warning. "Now, be a good girl and go sit down while I sweep up."

Stacy clamped her teeth together and sauntered over to the sofa, secretly relieved to collapse and rest her weary body.

"I'm ready to get back out," Drew said as he returned to the men.

"I'm with you." Bob rose. "Paul?"

"Yes," said Paul as he dragged himself to his feet.

Bob turned to Stacy. "Drew's team should get here in two or three hours. Until then, try to rest."

"Okay, Dad." Her voice softened. "Anything else I can do?"

"No. Thanks, anyway. We'll see you later."

"Bob, I'll drive," Drew offered as he strode over to the driver's side of the Jeep™.

Bob nodded briefly in agreement. Paul scrambled in back as Drew gunned the engine and the Jeep™ disappeared, hidden by a cloud of dust.

Stacy wandered back into the trailer, her mind involuntarily occupied by the perplexing man. His thoughtful consideration for her father was the antithesis of his condescending treatment of her.

"What a male chauvinist!" she mused. "But thank goodness I don't have to put up with him much more."

Stacy tossed restlessly on her narrow bed; her eyelids fluttered open. The early afternoon sunlight was streaming through the open window blinds. She realized that she must have dozed off. Abruptly, she sat up rubbing the sleep from her eyes.

The whine of large diesel engines could be heard through the thin walls of the trailer, alerting her to the imminent arrival of Drew's crew and equipment. She swung her legs off the bed and rose groggily. Within seconds she regained her equilibrium. She smoothed down the bright yellow gingham blouse, tucking the tails into the snug-fitting waistband of her jeans. The outfit clung closely to the supple curves of her youthful figure. Stacy quickly retied a bow in her hair to bring a bit of order to her unruly chestnut curls. Although the style was efficiently practical, it revealed the firm graceful lines of her cheeks and throat.

Two dusty blue trucks, branded with the white letters of Drew Pitman's company logo, stopped directly in front of the trailer as Stacy flung open the door. Hurriedly stepping down, she was met by a stocky crewman with a ruddy complexion.

With her normal self-assurance, Stacy introduced herself, adding, "My father and Mr. Pitman are waiting for you at the oil rig. I'll show you the way."

The crewman spoke with a classical east Texas twang. "Well, thanks, little lady. I'm John Mitchell, and that there is Mark Jefferies. Come on along."

Without giving him a second to reconsider, Stacy scrambled up in the cab and slammed the door shut.

In no time John had the truck lumbering along the rutted dirt track. While Stacy was sure he was a serious-minded fire-fighter, she was amused as he kept his eyes more on her than on the road.

Stacy glanced out the window and caught her reflection in the side mirror. Looking more closely, she suddenly realized that her blouse was gaping open; several buttons had worked themselves loose. She blushed crimson and unobtrusively turned sideways to furtively rebutton her shirt. As she leaned back in her seat, she was hard pressed to control a chuckle when she noticed both men's earnest concentration on the road ahead.

The hours of waiting had taken their toll; now Stacy felt compelled to witness firsthand the desperate battle at the rig. One-quarter mile from the well, the black smoke and unnaturally heated air stung her face and she immediately gained a personal appreciation for the men who had worked day and night under these torturous conditions. The sulfurous smell alone almost overpowered her.

Until an investigation was completed, the fire's exact cause would not be known, but it was generally believed to have been started by sparks from a faulty generator igniting the crude oil which had blown out when the drilling mud was too thin for the unexpected high pressure. As Stacy understood it, the emphasis now was on capping the well and thus eliminating the fire's supply of fuel.

Drew, standing with Bob, watched the truck's arrival with obvious disapproval. He climbed onto the running board and, leaning in through the window, demanded, "What in God's name are you doing here? This place is too dangerous for a woman—especially one who doesn't have any common sense."

Her wide brown eyes held a mute appeal as they locked on his tight angry features. Her position was indefensible, but she decided to brazen it out. "I couldn't just sit around twiddling my thumbs!"

Stacy's last shred of confidence deserted her as Drew's expression tightened. His knuckles, clenching the window frame, turned white as he considered his options. Stacy had correctly assumed that he could not spare the time or a crewman to drive her home, and he probably did not trust her enough to let her go on her own.

In a terse voice he barked, "Stay here and don't you dare move. We don't have any time to waste."

Stunned by his vehemence, Stacy remained silent.

"Can I trust you?"

"Yes, Mr. Pitman," she agreed meekly, secretly pleased that she had been permitted to stay for the final moments.

Drew darted her a suspicious glance, distrusting her

easy capitulation. "Just remember what I said," he returned darkly. Then without further comment he turned his attention to the men gathered around the trucks and instructed them on the requisite details.

Stacy sat wide eyed, absorbing all of the meticulous preparations. Everything set, Drew and two assistants were helped into fireproof suits. Protective water hoses were trained on them to reduce the blistering heat as they walked into the inferno to set the explosive charges. The charges were to be placed so that their detonation would cut off the air supply which fed the flames. Then armed with extinguishers and guarding against reignition, the men would cap the well to stop the escaping flow of gas and oil.

Stacy fixed her eyes on the blaze and breathed a prayer for the brave men; her watch ticked steadily as minutes dragged past. A deep sigh trembled from her lips when at last she saw three bulky forms emerging in blackened asbestos suits. Moments later the air was split by a rapid series of sharp explosions. As suddenly as the fire had started, the flames were gone. Men and equipment advanced and within five minutes the well was capped.

The valiant men stripped off their air packs and protective clothing. Stacy spotted Drew unharmed; his tan chiseled face was flushed, the sweat-soaked shirt stuck to his chest and arms, revealing his muscular build.

"Thank God they are safe!" she said, whispering her gratitude. Her eyes glistened with tears of happiness.

After receiving congratulations from Bob and his men, Drew approached the truck and his feminine audience. He cracked a boyish smile as he perceived her undisguised relief.

Drew reaffirmed the obvious. "It worked!"

"That was terrific!"

"Just shows what good teamwork can do," he answered, giving well-deserved credit to his crew.

Stacy admired his modesty, but she concealed these feelings and said, "You're lucky to have such a crew."

"Yep. Wouldn't be without them." He wiped the sweat from his brow. "Sure could go for a tall cold drink right about now."

"We have cold beer back at the trailer," offered Stacy.

"What are we waiting for? Let's go!"

Drew threw open the cab door and stood by and watched while Stacy hopped down. She practically ran to keep up with Drew as he strode over to a Jeep™. Without a moment's hesitation he grasped her around the waist and neatly lifted her inside.

Stacy plunked herself down in the seat, flustered by the intimate contact. "It wasn't necessary for you to manhandle me!"

Drew lifted an expressive eyebrow. "I thought we were in a hurry."

Stacy gave up. Then she looked around. "Where's Dad?"

"He'll be along in a few minutes."

Not at all certain she wanted to be alone with this unpredictable man, Stacy continued her questions. "What's keeping him?"

"He has to get things organized for the clean-up."

"Can't it wait?"

"Not with a storm on its way."

"I suppose you're right," she conceded, annoyed with herself for not realizing the obvious answer.

"Of course." He threw her a winning smile.

Not without effort, Stacy's pride forced her to resist his magnetism.

The Jeep's™ front wheels churned up a fine layer of dust, spreading it over the occupants. Stacy turned away from the window to avoid its full effect. The breeze caught her mane of chestnut hair, fanning it around her face like a veil. Even the dust and sweat could not camouflage its flaming highlights.

Stacy yielded to an irresistible urge and she covertly watched Drew through the protection of her thick brown lashes. She found herself unwillingly admiring his dexterity while he effortlessly guided the vehicle over the rutted track. Her eyes slowly edged up the length of his lean, muscular frame and cautiously examined his profile; fine lines radiated from the corner of his eye and a deep groove creased his cheek between his nose and the edge of his mouth. The sensuously full lower lip was in sharp relief to the narrow upper one.

Stacy was unconsciously lured on by the man's appeal. She speculated on how it would feel to be held tenderly by those powerful arms and kissed with that passionate mouth. As the thought crystallized, she contemptuously dismissed it and spent the remaining minutes berating herself for being so easily beguiled.

Drew eased the Jeep™ into a spot under a live oak tree across from the trailer, and before Stacy could recall herself to the present, he was at her side. She tried to ignore his extended hand, but he deftly grasped her arm when she stepped down. She unavoidably brushed against his body as her feet touched the ground, and shaking off his arm, she bolted away into the trailer.

Unruffled, Drew strolled over to the steps and paused under the awning. Stacy returned to the doorway and held out an ice-cold can of beer. "Would you like a couple of sandwiches?" she offered, once more composed now that there was several feet of space between them.

After taking a long swig of beer, Drew rubbed his

hand across the back of his neck. "What I'd really like is a hot shower."

"Help yourself. Your suitcase is by the door. You can use the bedroom on the left. Fresh towels are hanging in the bathroom."

"Thank you for your hospitality, ma'am."

His overly polite response irritated his hostess, but she returned evenly, "No trouble at all."

Drew carried his soft leather suitcase into the bedroom. Minutes later he reappeared clad in a terry-cloth robe and disappeared into the shower.

Stacy ignored the splashing water and trained her attention on preparing a plate of meat sandwiches. Then she searched the pantry for pickles and mustard; she eventually spotted them on the top shelf. With a weary sigh, she got a dinette chair and balanced her feet on the narrow seat.

As Stacy reached up to grasp the pickle jar, she was startled by a screech behind her. Spinning around to identify the strident sound, she yelped as she lost her balance. Arms automatically stretched out to break her fall, but instead of crashing onto the hard linoleum, Stacy's groping hands met the rough fabric of Drew's robe. She was caught up against his solid chest and took a trembling breath; her nostrils filled with the scent of clean damp skin and a woodsy after-shave lotion.

"You should be more careful," said Drew softly.

"You . . . you startled me," she weakly defended. The strong arms lifted her up and effortlessly carried her to the sofa.

"Are you hurt?"

"No . . . not at all."

"Is this becoming a habit?"

"What?"

"Rescuing you."

"What a nerve! If you hadn't surprised me by opening that blasted door, it never would have happened!" she accused rashly.

Drew's hands clasped her shoulders gently. "Calm down before you say something you'll regret."

"Don't tell me what to do!" Stacy retorted impulsively. Far from calm, her body was intensely aware of burning sensations aroused by fingers gently massaging her shoulders. Lowering her eyes to hide their expression, she now found herself viewing the tanned column of his throat and the curling mat of blond hair exposed by the gaping lapels of his robe.

"Take it easy. That is no way to reward me." His voice was soft but gently mocking.

Stacy's eyes flew up; a smile hovered on his taunting lips.

"What . . . do you mean?" she stammered.

"This."

Rising to his feet, he drew her stunned, unresisting body up with him and slid his arms around her back. He tightened his hold; his rock-hard muscles pressed against her soft curves. Stacy's breath was shallow—somewhere in the recesses of her mind a warning bell was frantically ringing; but her exhausted brain was too befuddled to heed its message.

At first he pressed his taut lips lightly against her tender mouth, but as they touched, some basic instinct spurred him on. The kiss deepened . . . both unexpectedly lost to the world around them.

A door slammed.

Drew released the bemused girl slowly, but he kept one sinewy arm securely across her slim shoulders as he faced the intruders: Bob Davidson and Paul Elmwood!

Stacy, writhing under their condemning inspection, blushed fiercely and tried to move away from Drew, but his arm was clamped on her shoulders. Her rosy color deepened as she registered the shock and dismay on both faces.

"What's going on here?" The censorious note was unmistakable in her father's voice.

Before she could find her voice, Stacy heard Drew announce smoothly, "You are the first to know; Stacy and I are engaged."

They're the first to know, all right! Stacy's mind balked at his presumption. She glanced at the men; surprise registered on Paul's face, while her father's expression visibly lightened.

"Well, well. Stacy, Drew, this comes as quite a surprise. I had no idea you even knew each other," said Bob pleasantly.

Drew adroitly fielded his question. "Stacy and I have known each other for some time, but until now I thought she was too young to know her own mind."

Stacy restrained a gasp at his audacity. He threw her a wicked smile as he continued, "I hope we haven't shocked you."

With tremendous willpower Stacy regained her poise and opened her mouth to refute Drew's tale before things got out of control.

Anticipating her action, Drew squeezed her shoulder warningly and added, "She's made me very happy."

"That's fine. You're a lucky man." Bob smiled warmly at his daughter.

Stacy, watching the men as Drew talked, realized that the announcement had truly pleased her father. Paul, on the other hand, was looking morose. She wondered why, but her attention was caught again as Drew ad-libbed: "Stacy, you should have told your father that we were dating when you were in secretarial school."

She felt like screaming or stamping her foot, preferably on his instep. *How brazen can he get!* she stormed silently. *He's complacently fabricating an entire affair. Next thing I know, he'll start naming places where we went on dates! Well, we'll just see about that!*

Aloud she said, "Yes, dear, you're 'right,' of course. I'm afraid I didn't mention it to Daddy because he was away at the time." Two could play this game.

She felt a sharp pinch on her arm reprimanding her glib retort, but Stacy was not repentant. She was too angry and frustrated by his inventiveness. Suddenly, it flashed in her mind that she had no acceptable explanations for being found in a half-clad stranger's arms. Her face flushed as she reflected on her potential embarrassment had Drew not stepped in with his deception. After all, an engagement did not have to be permanent . . . did it?

Drew ruefully glanced down at his robe and excused himself. "I'll change while you finish rustling up some food." He kissed her cheek chastely. Then using his body as a shield, he hissed in Stacy's ear, "Don't spoil it now!" Loud enough for the others to hear, he added, "Back in a minute, sweetheart." Then he turned and walked back to the bedroom.

Paul muttered forlornly, "Congratulations, Stacy," before he stalked out, letting the door slam behind him.

Now that they were alone, Bob enfolded his only daughter in his arms, hugging her securely. Then holding her at arm's length, he added his good wishes. "You've got yourself a fine man. I'm very happy for you, kitten."

Appalled by the magnitude of their deceit, Stacy stammered, "Th-thanks, Dad. I . . . I'm sorry we kept it a secret." Guilt swept over her.

"That's okay, kitten. I know it's been hard for you without a woman to confide in." His face clouded over momentarily as he thought of his wife, who had died five years earlier, just after her daughter completed high school.

Stacy's eyes misted. "You're the best father ever!" she declared, returning his embrace.

"Thanks, kitten. We'll talk more later. I need to get out of these clothes. Back in a minute."

"Okay." She turned back to her preparations and absolutely refused to worry about her current predicament. She'd let Drew handle it; after all, he'd started it! All this over one little kiss. Well, maybe not so little, she admitted honestly to herself. Her pulse quickened at the memory of those moments in his arms. No more! She sternly remonstrated herself. Then her sense of humor surfaced as she contemplated two grown men trying to dress in an area about as big as the proverbial postage stamp.

A chuckle bubbled up and escaped her lips.

"I'm glad you can find something to laugh about."

Stacy spun around to face Drew's narrowed gaze. With a mischievous smile she said, "Oh . . . I was just wondering how you and Dad were managing in that tiny bedroom."

The corner of his mouth lifted. "Fortunately, I had about finished, or one of us might have gotten an eye poked out."

She laughed again and then her expression sobered. "What did he say?"

"'Bout what?" he returned blandly.

"The engagement!" Frustration dimmed the sparkle in her eyes.

"He congratulated me."

"That was nice of him," she said sarcastically.

His eyebrow lifted. "Watch your step, my girl. We're not out of the woods yet," he warned.

Stacy's temper flared. "I'm not 'your girl!'"

"He thinks you are," Drew said, casting his eyes in the direction of the bedroom. "So keep a tight rein on that nasty tongue of yours."

Stacy pivoted on her heel, picked up the sandwich plate, carried it to the table, and set it down with a decided thump. Out of the corner of her eye, she caught Drew's taunting expression; she willed herself to move calmly, refusing to afford him further amusement. She skirted around him, walking briskly over to the ice chest for beer. She then paused, asking in dulcet tones, "Would you please get the mustard and pickles down from the pantry?" She pointed to the top shelf.

He grasped a jar in each hand. Stacy could not read the strange expression on his face.

"So that's why you were perched on a chair." He let loose with a deep laugh. "Amazing how such simple things can complicate our lives." He laughed again and this time Stacy joined him.

When Bob returned he found them comfortably seated at the table indulging their healthy young appetites. His eyes lit up at the cans of beer, beads of moisture glistening on their sides. "Looks like you thought of everything, Stacy."

"I try."

For the next few minutes the only sound to be heard was that of teeth munching on ham, cheese, and lettuce sandwiches and the gurgle of beer sliding down parched throats.

After the mound of sandwiches had all but disappeared, the men discussed plans for the well. Stacy's mind drifted until she was suddenly recalled by her father's inquiry: "Have you set a date for the wedding?"

Stacy shifted uncomfortably, darting a look at Drew, who grinned boldly. "We haven't discussed a date."

Audaciously, he continued, "Stacy needs a little time to get used to the idea."

Oooooh . . . the impertinent, cocky wretch! Stacy seethed. Her eyes detected a twinkle glimmering in the deep blue orbs. *Just you wait, Drew Pitman! I'll get even somehow! The first round may be yours, but it's not over, not by a long shot!*

Chapter Two

With few tasks to occupy her time, Stacy lingered as she unpacked her last suitcase. Then leaving the empty leather case by the bedroom door, she walked back to the narrow bed to smooth the peach-colored spread and stepped back to admire the room. Her bedspread matched the window drapes, which contrasted gently with the celery-green pile carpet. The high gloss of the polished walnut furniture reflected the morning sunlight. Whenever they were out of town for an extended time, Stacy arranged for a cleaning service to thoroughly air and clean the apartment so all she had to do was the laundry when they returned.

Restlessly, she wandered over to the window and glanced unseeingly at the scene below. For the last week her thoughts had been chaotic, haunted by her last conversation with Drew. He had adroitly suggested that she take him to the air field, and she had agreed, knowing that they needed to discuss their predicament privately.

With a sigh Stacy recalled the sparring match which had begun as soon as they were out of the trailer. Drew had insisted on driving and she had immediately demanded to know why. He had answered shortly, "I'd rather drive."

Unsatisfied, Stacy started toward the driver's seat.

"Get in on the other side!" the low voice commanded.

"No!"

"Do as I say; you're wasting time."

"But I'll be driving on the way back."

"So," he drawled the word.

"I'll just have to switch over then."

"That's fine with me."

"Well, I want to drive." Her eyes glimmered with frustration.

"Too bad. I don't intend to let you."

Giving in ungraciously, Stacy climbed into the passenger's seat and plunked herself down. She studiously watched the landscape out her window as they drove away from the camp. The wind had dispersed the fire's black clouds and now the fields were bathed in the orange glow of the setting sun. The cool breeze brushed her face refreshingly. She realized grudgingly that she would lose any verbal battle with such an arrogant, conceited . . .

Drew's deep voice pierced her brooding. "I'm glad you finally conceded."

Stacy was ready to erupt with an angry retort, but forced herself to say rationally, "I refuse to continue with a senseless argument. As you said, it's a big waste of time."

Drew tilted back his blond head and laughed heartily. He glanced over to her and said with a chuckle,

"Typical. Women always want the last word." His eyes returned to the road; his expression sobered. "Calm your ruffled feathers, Stacy. I don't intend to hold you to that announcement, so you need not jump on everything I say. Until we can end it gracefully, we'll carry on with the pretense. Which means, my dear girl," he said, piercing her with his dark blue eyes, "that we must act like friends."

Uncertain of his meaning, Stacy twisted around to stare at him and instantly felt the powerful impact of his masculinity. She suppressed the sensual impressions his nearness evoked and queried, "What do you mean?"

He answered blandly, "When we are out in public, we should present a united front and not bicker."

She conceded his point, but then asked, "What motivated you to make such a preposterous announcement?"

Drew slanted a glance at her flushed countenance. "I had my reasons."

"Please enlighten me!"

"All in good time."

Stacy fumed while Drew negotiated a rough patch in the road. Then, as his attention eased, he said drily, "Would you rather I let your father and Paul think the worst . . .? When they walked in, you did not appear to be resisting."

She turned back to the window and tried to hide the flush his words created. "Thanks for reminding me."

"Sorry, that was a cheap shot. But hasn't it penetrated that pretty little head of yours what you'd be exposed to without an adequate explanation for our behavior?" He continued derisively, "I'm sure Paul is a fine, upstanding young man, but even he might get the wrong idea, and your position in a camp of lonely males would have become untenable."

Reluctantly, she acknowledged, "I guess you're

right," her voice barely above a whisper. In the past she had easily handled Paul's advances, and the other men had a "hands off" policy toward the boss's daughter. But that might all have changed if the word had spread that she was available.

It rankled deeply for Drew to be so accurate in his assessment, but there was still one facet that they had not touched upon.

"You saw how Dad took the news." She said tersely, "He's delighted. My father's been thinking for quite some time that I should marry and have a life of my own."

Not without sympathy, Drew responded, "I haven't known Bob long, but I respect the man. I don't relish deceiving him, but in the long run it's better this way. Later, when we're both back in Houston, we can break it off quietly." He paused and then continued: "The only real problem is if it spoils a budding romance for you."

Lost in thought, Stacy did not respond.

"What about Paul Elmwood?"

Bewildered, Stacy shot him a glance. "What about him?"

"Don't be naïve. My announcement upset Paul."

"Really?" Stacy said faintly.

"Yes, really," Drew mimicked mockingly. In his normal voice he continued: "Now you're being obtuse. Is Paul important to you?"

"No!" she denied vehemently. "He is just an old friend." In a more even tone she added, "I've always thought of Paul as . . . well, as a big brother."

"Poor 'old' Paul," Drew returned with a hint of sarcasm. "Is that what he thinks? I detected more than 'brotherly' concern."

Stacy bristled at his tone and retorted defensively, "That's your impression, and if you are right, then this will just help Paul realize that I don't reciprocate his feelings. Hopefully, he'll begin to look elsewhere."

"Well, then, that's an added benefit."

She marveled at the callousness of his voice, but then wondered how he profited by their pseudo-engagement. "What do you get out of all this?"

Drew responded with a light laugh. "You are underrating your charming company."

"Oh, come on, Drew. You don't seem to be the type to lack female 'companionship.' Besides, I'd say that you always have a good reason for everything you do," Stacy returned, unimpressed by his blarney.

Noting her mien with a discerning glance, he admitted, "You're right."

"I am?"

Drew ignored her interruption and continued: "My current . . . lady friend has become rather demanding, and this mock engagement will allow me some breathing room."

Stunned by his offhanded explanation, Stacy felt unaccountably hurt. She was appalled by his deliberate ruthlessness, but at the same instant she perceived that she was guilty of the same reasoning. Chagrined, she realized ruefully that to denounce his motives was like the pot calling the kettle black. Instead, she taunted, "I'm surprised that a man of your 'experience' should need such a ruse."

"I just use the opportunities that present themselves."

Just how smug can you get! Stacy silently berated him.

By the time they reached the landing field, Stacy's temper had slowly cooled, and now she was reluctantly aware that she would miss this man who had so abruptly entered her life.

With a flick of his wrist, Drew turned off the engine.

Leaning one arm on the steering wheel, he glanced at Stacy's despondent figure. "I'll call you next week when you're back in Houston, and we can set up our first 'date.' Our engagement should appear normal to the world."

"Okay," she answered dispiritedly, overwhelmed by the magnitude of their lies.

He sensed her depression and added comfortingly, "Don't worry. Everything will work itself out." Drew looked through the windshield to the west, noticing the clouds building up near the horizon. The wind had picked up and he could smell the approaching storm. Undaunted, he said casually, "I should make it back to Houston ahead of the rain."

"Isn't it dangerous to fly such a light plane in this kind of weather?" Stacy lifted her head to view the darkening sky.

"Possibly, if I had left any later." He leaned forward and firmly pressed a kiss on her soft, appealing mouth. It was over in an instant, but it left a warm impression on her tingling lips, which spread treacherously throughout her body.

Mentally chiding herself for responding to his practiced charm, Stacy watched anxiously as Drew strode over to the twin-engine plane. With a wave of his hand, he climbed into the cabin. Within minutes he had maneuvered the aircraft for takeoff. The engines revved up with a deafening roar and the light airplane moved forward with ever-increasing speed until it soared upward, flattening the coarse grass with its force.

The strident ringing of the telephone brought Stacy back to the present. She picked up the extension phone on the nightstand and sat down on the bed. "Hello."

"Hi, Stacy. How you doing?"

Stacy immediately recognized Drew's deep voice. "Just fine." She rushed on. "Dad and I got home last night."

"I know. I spoke with your father this morning."

"You did?"

"Yes. We had some business to discuss, and I've been asked to bring you to a party this evening."

"Tonight?"

"Yes. Mrs. Woodward asked that you both join us. She assures me that you are welcome. You'd have had a personal invitation had she known you'd be back in town. "The voice continued drolly, "She had word of our engagement."

Stacy took a deep breath. "How did she hear about it?"

"'Bout what?"

She did not hide her annoyance when she said, "The engagement, of course!"

"Good news travels fast. This is a good chance for us to be seen together."

Hesitating for a moment, Stacy wished that this charade had never begun. She hated deceiving so many people; everything was snowballing at an enormous rate. Soon all of their friends would know of the engagement, if they hadn't gossiped about it already. She had hoped to get through it quietly, but now she envisioned many complications. Well, she decided philosophically, the sooner it's begun, the quicker her life could return to normal. Unfortunately, that did little to comfort her.

"Can you be ready by six-thirty?" Drew's voice intruded.

"Yes, I can," she said briskly.

"This is just a cocktail party, so we'll have dinner afterwards."

"You need not go to the trouble."

"My pleasure." Then he added with a trace of amusement, "Don't you think your father would consider it strange if I brought you home at eight-thirty?"

Chagrined by her oversight, she admitted reluctantly, "Yes, of course."

"See you later, then. Bye."

"Bye, Drew." As she replaced the receiver she was startled by the tremor in her hand. *Even over the phone his forceful personality is affecting me!* Forcing these traitorous thoughts from her mind, she turned her attention to her closet. She vacillated over her choice and femininely decided to buy a new dress for the party.

Eager to go shopping, Stacy checked her appearance. Her hair was freshly washed and hung in loose curls around her shoulders, sunlight glistening on its burnished copper highlights. She added a stroke of lipstick and powdered her nose. Satisfied with the reflection in the dressing table's mirror, she tucked her wallet and keys into her saddle-brown handbag. She decided not to change the light wool pantsuit woven in a plaid of chocolate brown, beige, and gold with a matching silky gold blouse.

After leaving a note for her father, Stacy conscientiously locked the apartment door and scampered lightly down the steps to the sidewalk and headed for the Galeria, just two blocks away. She enjoyed the convenience of living so close to Houston's largest shopping mall. Most people overlooked this quiet little street. Both sides of the road were lined with apartment buildings. Grass, shrubs, and trees—live oak and mesquite—added to the charming atmosphere. Before crossing the main thoroughfare to the Galeria, Stacy passed the building on the corner in which Bob Davidson had his office.

She walked straight to Neiman-Marcus and took the escalator to the second-floor designer department. There she found the perfect dress: a silk organza dyed in swirls of coral, russet, and flaming red.

Ecstatic over her shopping success, Stacy slowly strolled along past the shops. She did not have nearly enough time to investigate even a small fraction of the stores lining the Galeria's three levels. But, as always, she paused by the railing to watch the figure skaters glide across the ice rink built in the ground level.

Conscious of her growing hunger, she moved on, but her eye was caught by a familiar figure gazing at a window display.

"Katie Goodwin! How good to see you!" Stacy's face lit up as she approached her childhood friend. "I thought you were working in Austin."

The other girl, on hearing her name, had turned in surprise and quickly smiled as she recognized Stacy. "Stacy, it's been too long." The girls exchanged a brief, joyful hug. Katie was several inches shorter than Stacy's five feet, six inches, and just as slim. Short, blonde curls emphasized the elfin features of her face, her turned-up nose, and dancing blue eyes.

The girls chatted for a few minutes before Stacy suggested they have lunch together. Katie instantly agreed and several minutes later they were seated beneath a brightly colored umbrella of a restaurant whose motif had the effect of a sidewalk café. After the girls ordered chef's salads, they continued their conversation.

During a brief lull, Stacy asked, "So tell me, what are you doing in Houston?" Before Katie could answer, she teased, "You aren't getting married, are you?"

Katie shook her head and laughed lightly. "Will you be serious? I'm a working girl! I quit the job in the law office last week. Since my father died last year, Mother

has been all alone, so I decided to move back home."
The color had left her face, belying the calm tone of
her voice.

Stacy, sensitive to her friend's grief, quickly offered
her sympathy and unsubtly changed the subject by
saying, "Have you found a new job?"

"Not yet. I've been back only a few days."

"Katie, why don't you apply for a job with the
company where Dad and I work?" Barely pausing for
breath, she added brightly, "They always need good
secretaries, and I know that one of the girls is leaving
soon to have her baby."

The mournful look had been erased, and Katie
became cheerful. "Do you think I could? I wouldn't
like to presume."

Stacy recalled how well Katie had done in secretarial
college, so she said honestly, "I know you would be
good at the job. Besides, you have experience now and
the references to prove it. I can assure you that you
would be hired on your own merits; the company does
not waste its money on anyone's friends. Just contact
Mr. Beltmore, the personnel manager."

Katie gave a decided nod with her head as she said,
"All right, I'll try it. Thanks, Stacy, for giving me the
lead." Then she eyed the dress box propped next to her
friend's feet. "Now you can answer my questions.
What's in the box? I'm dying to know what you bought
at Neiman's."

"A dress."

Katie's curiosity was obviously not satisfied, and
Stacy smiled as she watched her friend unsuccessfully
try to contain her interest.

"Is it for a special occasion?" she guessed, but then,
seeing the glint in Stacy's eyes, she knew that she was
being deliberately led on. "So give—where are you
going to wear it?"

Stacy eyed her friend carefully, wondering if she should confide in her the truth, but she finally decided against it, since it would not be fair to Drew. Unfortunately, Katie had known her well all through school when they were supposedly "dating," which meant Stacy had to be extra cautious. She plunged in: "Drew Pitman is taking me out to a cocktail party and to dinner afterward."

"Wow! How did you meet him?" Katie was impressed and did not notice the apprehensive glaze of Stacy's eyes. "I've read about him in the newspapers."

Still not out of the woods, Stacy answered carefully, trying to keep the facts vague enough not to arouse her friend's suspicions. "Actually, we dated briefly a while ago, and then last week he was called out to the site when there was a fire." Relief washed over her when Katie did not question it but asked instead, "Is he as good looking as his pictures?"

A vivid image of Drew focused in Stacy's mind as she found herself saying, "Yes, I believe he is, in a rugged sort of way. What I'd call a 'man's man'; he has a slight cleft in the center of his square chin, dark, velvet blue eyes, blond hair, and a deep tan even at this time of year." Abruptly the words died as Stacy caught her friend's speculative stare.

"You seem to know him very well." Stacy could feel the heat in her cheeks as Katie leaned forward to add, "Stacy, be very careful. Drew Pitman has quite a reputation. I don't want you to get hurt."

Overwhelmed by her deceit and Katie's endearing warning, Stacy's glance flickered away from Katie's clear blue eyes. She looked pointedly at her watch and made her excuses to leave. "I've got to run. Please keep in touch. Let me know how the interview goes." With a quick stop to settle the bill, Stacy was off with a wave of her hand.

Now oblivious to the scenery, the noise, and fumes from the traffic, Stacy walked swiftly back to the apartment. Slowing her pace, she realized that no matter how fast she went, she could not run away from her conscience.

After soaking for the better part of an hour in a tub of scented hot water, Stacy felt more relaxed and better able to cope with the perils of the evening ahead. She rose gracefully and briskly toweled herself dry before slipping into a soft, sage-green velour wrap robe. As she gave a final tug to the belt she heard the sound of the front door closing and heavy footsteps as her father entered the apartment.

By the time she reached the living room, Bob Davidson was comfortably ensconced in an easy chair with the evening paper spread open. He looked up as his daughter walked in and came to brush his lined cheek with an affectionate kiss. She noticed how tired he looked and said, "Hi, darling. Had a rough day?"

"No more so than usual."

Stacy perched on the arm of his chair and slid her hand across his shoulders. "Are you sure you feel up to going out this evening?"

A mysterious smile lit his face. "I wouldn't miss it for the world."

Still concerned, she asked, "Are you sure I can't get you anything? I could fix up a plate of cheese and crackers or something more substantial if you'd like."

"Quit fussing. I'll be fine. As a matter of fact, I'm not in the least hungry. I went out to eat for lunch and came back feeling stuffed. Any more food and I'll have another bout of indigestion."

"Are you ill?"

"No, not at all." He gave her a wry smile. "It's just at my age I can't eat all the rich foods I'd like."

Her face was still shadowed with concern.

"Look, you go finish getting ready. I want to read the paper for a few minutes before I change."

"Okay. But one last question."

His eyes twinkled. "Just like a woman."

She groaned softly as she remembered another man who had made the same comment, and said with spirit, "I'll ignore that since you're my father. I just wanted to know if you wanted to dine with Drew and me after the party."

"Thanks, but no, thanks. You and Drew don't need an old man like me tagging along. I'm content to have a quiet evening. It will give me a chance to finish reading the paper uninterrupted." His eyes twinkled up at her.

"Oh, you! I'm going!" She reached her other arm around to give him a swift hug before she slid to her feet and walked back to her room.

With a few minutes to spare, she flipped on her clock radio so she could listen to some music while she finished dressing.

Sitting at the dressing table, she carefully French-braided her hair, starting high on the crown. She wrapped the loose ends up and tucked them under and anchored them with bobby pins. The loose plaiting separated the layers of side and back hair, revealing the brilliant shades of her shining hair. For the final touch she twisted a tendril of hair at each ear.

Then she added subtle touches of eyeshadow, blusher, and lipstick coordinated with the crimson tones of her dress. She shrugged off her robe and tossed it over the end of the bed. The cool air caressed her bare skin for a moment as she selected appropriate undergarments from her dresser drawers. Then she slipped on the silky peach lingerie which felt sensuous against her creamy skin and stepped into the long, flowing dress. She reached back to close the zipper, but halfway up it snagged. Fruitlessly, she struggled with it for a few seconds before conceding defeat. Calling to her father, she followed sounds to the living room. Without bothering to hold the upper edges of the dress together, she went down the hallway. Suddenly, she jerked to a stop in the doorway, stunned by the presence of the tall man who was rising to his feet.

"Hello, Stacy. Your father told me to make myself at home." He raised a full glass, clinking with ice.

"Oh . . . good." She backed away. "I'll be ready in a minute."

Before she could retreat into the dimness of the hallway, Drew had moved with lightning speed to stand mere inches from her.

"May I be of help?" he asked with a mischievous grin.

Prepared to make a swift denial, she unconsciously straightened her shoulders. Then, with as much dignity as she could assume with the neckline of her dress sliding down her shoulders, she said, "I'll go find Dad . . . if you'll excuse me."

"Your father's in the middle of dressing." He continued mockingly: "Don't be so prudish; you're well covered." Authoritatively, he added, "Turn around."

With a resigned sigh, she turned around so he could examine the zipper. She shivered slightly as his lean fingers manipulated the twisted fabric. "Hold still!" Seconds later he slid the zipper closed.

"There, now, that wasn't so bad."

"Thanks," she murmured. Without another word, she turned and dashed back into the sanctuary of her room. Her heart was racing and her face was crimson from embarrassment.

For a moment she leaned against the closed door, trying to regain some degree of equanimity after the

devastating encounter. With just the slightest of touches, Drew had robbed her of all her normal self-
possession and she needed a few minutes before she
could face him with any degree of detachment. She
found it disconcerting to be so ruffled by a man she
hardly knew.

With an effort, she pushed herself away from the
door and completed the final touches to her
appearance—slipped on strappy, high-heeled shoes,
and added pierced earrings and a gold circlet around
her wrist. Femininely, she had hoped to use this
occasion to erase the sloppy tomboy impression of
her last encounter with Drew. But her transfigura-
tion had been marred by a drooping dress and bare
feet!

On the other hand, she thought he epitomized the
coolly sophisticated male, dressed as he was in a navy
blue vested suit with a pale gray silk shirt and crisply
knotted striped tie. It was a sharp contrast to the jeans
and work shirt of their first meeting, but he carried it
off with aplomb.

She left her bedroom carrying her short fur evening
jacket over her arm and clutching her silk purse.

Drew stood as she entered the living room and
sauntered over to take the jacket from her arm and
courteously held it until she slipped it on. With an
intimate squeeze of her shoulders, he said softly, his
breath caressing her right ear lobe, "You look lovely,
Stacy."

He straightened away from her and stepped back.
His eyes leisurely roamed down her body and back to
her face. Stacy's color heightened under his intimate
scrutiny. His mouth twisted into a smile as he said
drolly, "Quite a difference."

The flush deepened, but with a spark of resentment
she said, "I'm glad you approve."

"I certainly do," he countered with a suggestive glance at her shapely curves.

She glanced uneasily around the room. "Will Dad be ready soon?"

"Your father will meet us at the party."

"Oh, really? When did you decide this?"

"When I arrived. . . . All set?"

"I suppose so," she responded dispiritedly.

"Smile! We're going to a party, not an execution."

The words slipped out carelessly. "You could have fooled me."

He lifted one eyebrow and she said contritely, "Sorry. I guess I'm just nervous . . . meeting all these people."

"Take it easy. You know most of them." His deep voice was soothing, and Stacy had no choice but to precede him out the front door as he gestured her through with a gallant sweep of his arm.

Jumbled in her mind were niggling doubts about the evening ahead. Was it wise? This frequent exposure to such a blatantly virile male? Ultimately, would he . . .

Chapter Three

A short time later they were walking up the front sidewalk to a beautiful house the size of a mansion. The brick and the columns supporting the portico were painted white. A huge brass lantern illuminated the veranda. Lights blazed in every window. The early blooming wisteria perfumed the air.

Drew's fingers were locked with hers, and Stacy gained a certain strength from his support. Her mind balked at the ordeal ahead.

The brief ride in his black Corvette had been relatively uneventful. Drew had silently concentrated on steering the low-slung car through heavy traffic while Stacy had gazed out the window, trying her best to ignore her reaction to the vital man inches away. But this had failed. Every time she felt her dress stir as his hand brushed the fabric as he changed gears of the four-speed stick shift. She was relieved when it was time to leave the intimate confines of the car. He had taken her hand to help her out of the low leather bucket seat, and then he had kept hold of it as they strolled to the house.

The front door was immediately opened by a uniformed maid who directed Stacy to leave her jacket in an upstairs bedroom set aside for the ladies' use.

With a last-minute check in the antique mirror of the dressing table, she straightened her shoulders and steeled herself to face the curiosity and surprise of the people below.

Halfway down the curving staircase her heel caught in the plush carpeting. As her left hand grasped the mahogany banister, her right was taken in an iron grip.

"Careful, now, it wouldn't do to tumble down these stairs."

"Drew, where did you come from?" Stacy said, startled by his sudden appearance at her side.

"What? No thanks for saving you from an undignified entrance?"

"Thanks."

"That will do. There are too many people watching us. Now, smile, you're supposed to be happy. A woman newly engaged to a terrific catch."

Stacy found herself smiling at his blatant self-mockery.

"That's better. Come on. They're waiting for us."

He continued his firm grasp of her hand as they stepped down to the hall. The center of the terrazzo flooring was covered with a large Oriental rug woven with gorgeous yarns, ranging in shades from powder to royal blue. Touches of rose, cream, and gold added to its elegance. A sparkling crystal chandelier dominated the hallway. Its light danced through glass prisms onto the ivory walls.

Before Stacy could gain more than an impression of the large, beautifully proportioned and decorated living room, she and Drew were swallowed up by the crowd of people filling it.

Their hostess, Mrs. Woodward, an imposing grey-haired matron, made her way through the clusters of people to greet them warmly. She grasped their free hands in each of hers.

"Stacy and Drew, I'm so glad you could be here."

Stacy murmured an appropriate response, while Drew said, "Thank you for inviting us."

"Stacy, dear, you look charming."

"Thank you, Mrs. Woodward, but I could never compete with you."

The older woman laughed lightly. "That's nice of you to say, dear," she said. Then with a suggestive glance in Drew's direction, she added, "But we know who appeals to this young man, don't we?"

"I'm sure your husband is relieved," Drew teased.

"Oh, you." Her eyes sparkled.

Their light banter continued until their hostess left them to continue with her duties.

Drew adjusted Stacy's hand so it rested in the crook of his arm; her fingers curled into his jacket sleeve.

Their progress through the richly appointed room was halted several times. Drew skillfully made any necessary introductions, easing Stacy into her role as his fiancée. She kept a bright smile and carefully fielded the inquiries which came her way.

Stacy noticed that in every case Drew charmed the ladies. Several of them gave her sidelong looks which were obviously tinged with envy. And yet with the men he had an equal, if not greater, appeal. As she had told Katie, he was a man's man.

After several minutes, Drew excused both of them so they could partake of the refreshments. Once they were away from the throng, Drew said, "You did that very well."

"What?" Stacy was baffled by his comment and looked up into his face to see an unfathomable expression in his eyes.

"Play the adoring fiancée," he gibed.

She responded somewhat tartly, "Isn't that what I'm here for?"

"Of course. Keep up the good work," he taunted.

Stacy was confused. Since they had arrived, he had seemed to be making things as pleasant as possible for her under the circumstances, and she had been relieved to find everything had been going so smoothly. She had felt some trepidation at publicly facing the consequences of his precipitous announcement. Now he seemed to be cynical, condemning the very thing he had wanted her to do.

"What would you like to eat? Do you need a fresh drink?"

His voice pulled Stacy back to the present and she faced a table filled with a variety of hors d'oeuvres and small, dainty sandwiches filled with cream cheese, tuna, and chicken salad. And for fish lovers, there were fresh shrimp cocktail and even black caviar.

Stacy wrinkled her nose as the pungent aromas assailed her. Suddenly she did not feel up to eating anything. Her stomach was churning from nervous tension.

"Oh, I'm not very hungry."

"Try something. It will make you feel better." He had switched back again to solicitude, and Stacy shrugged mentally, deciding that she would never be able to understand this enigmatic man. He was a law unto himself.

"I think you'll enjoy the sandwiches. The other is rather spicy."

"Thanks." She reached for a plate from the stack of bone china at the end of the table, but before she could grasp it, his body blocked her and he handed her the one he had been quietly filling.

"I can get my own, thank you."

"I do not want to argue with you, so please take it." The command in his voice could not be ignored, but Stacy gave it a try.

"I prefer to serve myself."

"Sure you do, but this once accept my gracious offering."

She felt chagrined, took hold of the plate, and quietly stepped back to wait as he piled another plate with food.

"Why don't we sit over there while we eat?" He motioned to two rather comfortable-looking uphol-stered velvet wing chairs set near the fireplace.

"Fine." The guests in this end of the room had melted away, so they were able to relax for a few minutes as they ate. Stacy only nibbled at her food, silently wishing he had not given her so much. She hated waste, and whenever she left food on a plate she remembered all the starving people of the world who could have benefited by it.

She had just decided she couldn't eat another bite when she spotted her father talking with their host, an urbane-looking man, just inside the doorway. Tom Woodward was motioning his guests for silence as Bob indicated with a glance and a wave of his hand that he wanted Drew and Stacy to join them.

Stacy hesitated a moment, but then Drew was at her side, taking the plate from her to set it on a convenient table before grasping her by the elbow and propelling her forward. Puzzled by what was happening, Stacy glanced at the faces of the other guests. They seemed to be waiting expectantly. Before she could form a question, she heard her father say proudly, "I am pleased to announce the engagement of my daughter,

Stacy, to Drew Pitman. I hope you'll join me in wishing them every happiness."

Her eyes had misted over at the warmth and pride evident in her father's voice, but she was stunned when the announcement fully penetrated her mind. Quickly she schooled her features to smile, her lips curved up, but it did not quite reach her eyes. Stacy flicked a glance up at Drew's face. He did not appear at all surprised, and she wondered curiously why. No one had mentioned to her that he would make a public announcement this evening.

She felt a movement at her side as Drew released her arm to reach his hand into his jacket pocket. It came out with a tiny jeweler's box partially concealed by his long fingers. She found her carefully controlled poise disintegrating as he nonchalantly pressed the catch to open the box, revealing an exquisitely cut oval diamond solitaire set in a yellow-gold band. She gasped.

In a low voice only she could hear, Drew said, "Take it easy. What's an engagement without a ring?"

Equally softly, Stacy murmured, "It's beautiful. But this is too much!"

He ignored her comment and gently removed the ring from its velvet bed. He reached for her left hand and had to hold it steady as he gently slipped the ring on her third finger. "Your father told me your ring size."

She raised wide eyes to his. "It's perfect," she breathed.

"Good." Without another word he bent his head and kissed her lips, pressing his mouth into hers as his hands slid around her shoulders, drawing her close. Stacy reveled in their warmth, her treacherous body instantly responding to his touch. She forgot everything as she allowed her lips to be molded by his.

The spell was broken when Drew raised his head and turned to listen to the congratulations from the friends who were surrounding them. Stacy felt herself instantly catapulted back to reality. As she looked up, her velvet brown eyes caught a young woman's malevolent expression. She was standing a little apart from the crowd: flawlessly groomed, brassy hair pulled back in a sophisticated topknot emphasizing her strong cheekbones, and dressed in a modern gown of ice blue. The color of the dress matched her eyes. Their icy paleness enhanced the feeling of animosity Stacy found radiating from her. As she watched, the woman sauntered over, her eyes focused on Stacy's face.

Turning to Drew for an explanation, Stacy realized that during the intervening moments he had been drawn away from her side by some boisterous friends. When the stranger stood directly in front of her, Stacy forced herself to meet her cool gaze with one of her own.

"Congratulations, Miss Davidson." The voice was as chilly as her eyes.

"Thank you. I don't believe we've met."

"That's right. I'm Jennifer Hyatt."

She did not bother to extend her chalk-white hand.

Stacy maintained her poise and said politely, "It's nice to meet you."

"I'm sorry I can't say the same," Jennifer almost sneered.

Bewildered by the enmity obvious in her voice and manner, Stacy was at a loss for words.

"You may think you have him, but Drew will soon tire of your juvenile charms," Jennifer said insultingly.

Stacy flung back her head as though physically struck. Then her innate strength bolstered her. "I refuse to continue this." Without another word, she ignored the other woman's open-mouthed astonishment and pivoted on her heel. She walked over to stand beside Drew, wishing she could slip into his arms and draw upon his strength.

Drew looked down, noting the glazed eyes and pallor of her skin. "Ready to leave?" She was only able to nod her head in response and quickly found herself being led from the roon. A maid fetched her jacket, and once it was on, they paused only long enough to say thank you and good night to Bob and the Woodwards. Then Drew grasped Stacy's elbow and steered her to the front door.

As the heavy door thudded behind them, Stacy paused to take a deep breath. The cool evening air was a refreshing change from the stuffy, overpowering blend of perfume and cigarette smoke inside.

After a minute she felt better, her color returning with the easing of the tension stimulated by the obnoxious Miss Hyatt.

"I'm hungry. Let's go get dinner," Drew suggested.

The churning of her stomach still had not ceased, but Stacy agreed. "Fine. I hope it's quiet. I'm not ready for another crowd."

"Just what I had in mind," he returned. "I hope you enjoy French cooking. My reservations are for a place operated by a Frenchman. His standards are high and he personally trains and supervises all his staff."

"Sounds delightful. There are so many good restaurants in town, but so many offer the same thing—steak, seafood, or Mexican food."

"Sometime I'll take you to a little Mexican place that I know. It's run by a family and you get the real thing there, not some Americanized version. But tonight I thought we needed someplace quiet where we can relax."

"Thanks. I can go for that."

"I thought so," he drawled.

"Don't you ever get tired of being right?" she said smartly.

"Nope." The flash of strong white teeth was illuminated by the moonlight. "Let's stop talking and get going. It'll take us about twenty minutes to get there."

He opened the door and she eased herself into the car. Stacy felt more of her tension float away as she relaxed in the comfortable seat, deliberately forcing herself to keep her mind blank, but ever aware of the strong, silent man beside her.

"You're very quiet," Drew said with a quick shift of his eyes in Stacy's direction. "Are you tired?"

"Not really." She clasped her hands to control their involuntary tremor and felt the diamond dig into her right palm. She glanced down, spreading her fingers. The streetlights caught in the many facets and made it twinkle. Suddenly, she felt depressed; this charade had gone way beyond her. Now, as well as the guilt she felt for deceiving everyone, especially her father, she had been entrusted with a valuable ring which she did not want. Compelled to make things clear, she turned her body sideways to face Drew and said, "I wish you hadn't bought such a valuable ring."

"Don't worry about it," Drew responded easily.

"But I am," she said stiffly. "I want you to know I'll take good care of it until it's time for me to give it back."

"I don't want it back."

"But I can't keep it!"

"Why not?"

"Because it wouldn't be right! I don't know much about jewelry, but even I know it wasn't cheap, and there's no need for you to be out such a large amount of money." She paused for breath. "It's one thing for you to take me out to dinner, but quite another to buy me jewelry."

Drew let her finish without interruption. Then, as they were stopped at a traffic light, he turned and his blue eyes pierced her. "It's an engagement ring."

"I realize that, but this is not a real engagement," she said incautiously, losing her patience with his attitude.

"It is until I decide differently."

"You decide!" Her voice rose higher.

He coolly glanced at the traffic lights and shifted gears, picking up speed. She slumped back in her seat, frustrated by his stand and unable to argue while he was driving.

The seconds ticked away. Drew's deep voice broke the silence, but he kept his eyes on the traffic. "Let's shelve this discussion. For now, we're in this situation for better or worse . . . forgive the pun. We can decide what to do with the ring later." He continued patiently: "I can't return it, and I can't imagine giving it to another woman, but maybe we'll come up with a reasonable solution later."

Stacy sighed. It was not the answer she wanted, but she decided that any further discussion would be fruitless.

Not many minutes later, the car turned into a shopping center built like a small village constructed in sandstone; it gave the area an Old-World charm, not unlike a European village. The restaurant, built like a mill with a water wheel, was set off at one corner, and opposite it was a tall clock tower; the intervening space was occupied by more shops and a landscaped parking area.

As they entered the restaurant they were greeted by the maître d' and ushered to a linen-draped table for two.

Silver and crystal glistened with the reflected light from the wall sconces. The entire room had a subdued elegant atmosphere; oyster-white walls were trimmed with molding painted the color of green Wedgwood china, and the thick, plush carpeting was of a darker green hue. A mural of paintings of famous landmarks in Paris covered one wall.

Now thirsty, Stacy asked for a *piña colada* while Drew ordered a Scotch on the rocks. The menu offered a wide selection, but ultimately they chose veal cutlets to be served with a sauce of chopped ham, mushrooms, and delicate seasonings; and with it they ordered a Sauterne wine.

Stacy sipped her ice cooled drink, letting the icy concoction slide down her parched throat. Suddenly, she sensed Drew's eyes on her and lifted her own to read the expression in their blue depths.

She smiled, lifting the corners of her mouth, and, unaware of the sparkle in her eyes, involuntarily was pleased to be out in his stimulating company. She felt his gaze caress her brow and cheeks, and as it rested on her parted lips she was overwhelmed by bewildering sensations. Deliberately, she dropped her lashes to hide her confusion, disconcerted by his instant effect on her senses.

She started to say something, anything to break the spell, when the waiter returned with their appetizer of hot onion soup.

"You'll enjoy this, Stacy. I always find it excellent."

She took a spoonful. Abruptly, the image of Jennifer Hyatt popped into her mind and Stacy wondered if Drew had ever brought her here. She unsuccessfully tried to phrase a question, but anything she could say Drew might interpret as being too possessive or petty. Sooner or later she would discover more about the haughty woman. Stacy had already deduced that

Jennifer was the "lady friend" Drew was trying to discourage.

Aloud, she said, "It is delicious. I wish I had more time to cook like this, but with Dad and me working, we rely heavily on convenience foods."

"Maybe you'll have more time after you are married," suggested Drew tauntingly.

"Only if I quit my job," she said logically.

"Then marry someone who can support you without your needing to work," he parried.

"Like you," she said, being deliberately provocative. She refused to allow him to get the upper hand.

"Or someone like me," he countered smoothly.

She thought seriously for a moment. "I don't know that I'd like to give up my career."

"Isn't marriage a career?"

"It is for some women. I'll just have to wait and see," she concluded lightly as the waiter returned to remove their dishes.

With the assistance of another man, a specially designed serving cart was rolled over by the waiter. Then, as Stacy watched, fascinated by the swift movements, sliced tomatoes and green beans were lightly tossed as they were cooked in a skillet. When ready, they were turned out onto china plates kept warm by a heating element. Then the sauce was mixed and poured over the veal. In a very short time they were set before Drew and Stacy.

Once the waiters left, Stacy ate with gusto the delicately spiced food, a treat for her palate. As the hunger pangs, created by the delicious aromas enticing her nostrils, were assuaged, she searched her mind for a topic of conversation. Finally, falling back on the time-old solution, she asked, "Tell me something about your work. Does it take you very far?"

With a mocking smile, he said, "Do you really want

to know, or is this just a ruse to keep me from questioning you?"

Stacy flushed slightly at his perception but asserted staunchly, "I'd like to know. Don't forget—through my father I've been interested in another aspect of the oil business for years."

"Touché!" His eyes searched her face and then, as if satisfied with what he found, he continued: "Since there are many oil fields in the Southwest, I usually work here, but sometimes I'm called into a foreign country. Good old American know-how is respected internationally." He paused to take a bite of food. "We've been drilling since oil was first discovered in Pennsylvania in 1859, and dealing with its hazards. Now that modern technology has facilitated drilling in obscure places, there is an even greater demand for trained people to handle the problems. Mexico and Great Britain, for example, are just beginning to develop their oil reserves. The offshore drilling platforms the English need to use in the North Sea have unique problems."

"It's amazing, isn't it, how engineers and scientists have come up with methods to suit almost any environmental situation? My father has had to work in some places where the oil is thick and difficult to pump. But once someone discovered it could be thinned by heating it with steam, it is now accessible."

They continued with their meal, their conversation revolving around the oil business. As time passed Stacy found herself answering questions about her personal life.

"You're very close to your father." It was more a statement than a question.

Stacy knew that in this day and age the "older generation" usually was not very popular with their young, but she had a very special relationship with her father and enjoyed working with him. She said honestly, "Yes, since Mother died, I've tried to keep him from getting too lonely." There was a catch in her voice as she added, "They were very close. It was a crushing blow when she died." She blinked back the tears blurring her vision.

Drew's voice came through warm and sympathetic. "They were very fortunate. Few people are so blessed."

"Yes," she whispered, wondering if she would ever be so lucky. She was dumbfounded to realize that she had carried the thought a step further and was actually thinking about how it would be to be loved by a man like Drew. Instantly, she chided herself. Drew had no permanent place in her life, and she would be a fool if she let herself be bowled over by his dynamic personality.

She was brought back to the present as Drew shifted the conversation to more neutral channels.

While they were sipping their after-dinner coffee, Drew said, "We don't want doubts about the sincerity of our engagement, so while I'm in town I'll be taking you out." He raised a hand to halt her interruption. "I travel a lot so you needn't see much of me. Besides, when we do go out there's no reason we can't have a good time." Baffled by her irrational disappointment at his cold-blooded words, she let him continue uninterrupted.

"Are you free tomorrow afternoon?"

"Yes," she murmured.

"Good. Wear something casual."

Her curiosity was piqued and she asked, "Where are we going?"

"Wait. Let it be a surprise," he said with a tantalizing note in his voice.

He's done it again, she thought, furious with herself

for her obvious show of interest. *Well, I can be just as cool as he is!* Aloud, she said, "Good. That should please my father."

Drew raised an eyebrow but said nothing more.

He signaled for the check. It was summarily dealt with and they left.

It was not long before they were back at Stacy's apartment. Instead of following Stacy up the steps to her front door, he pulled her gently by the hand through the arched walkway which led to the apartment's inner courtyard.

Inside, the night was still. Their footsteps on the brick walk and the light tinkling of a fountain were the only sounds to break the silence. Stacy could smell earthy scents created by the dew-moistened vines and shrubs.

She found her voice. "Why are we here?"

Drew stopped and took her by the shoulders to turn her to face him. "This evening is too lovely to end so soon."

She hesitated, her eyes trying to read his expression in the moonlight. With an attempt at remaining aloof, she answered, "It has to end sometime."

"But it's not over yet," he murmured, slowly lowering his head to graze her cheek with his tantalizing lips. She could not remain unaffected as he brought her soft body against his hard unyielding frame; his lips fired her body as they trailed down her face to her mouth, which parted under his insistent pressure. Her hands had moved of their own volition up under his jacket to massage the taut muscles of his back.

All too soon the night air was between them. Drew stooped to pick up Stacy's purse, which had fallen unnoticed to the pavement. Handing it to her, he took her arm and escorted her out of the courtyard and up the steps to her door. Stacy fumbled with the purse

until she located her keys buried in the bottom. In an
instant Drew had plucked them from her fingers and
unlocked the door.

Once she had stepped inside, he closed the door
behind her with a quick good night. Stacy could hear
his jaunty tread down the stairs and wondered how she
could steel herself against his overwhelming appeal in
the days ahead.

Chapter Four

It was past mid-morning when Stacy arose. After shrugging on a robe, she went in search of her father. She found him in the dining room, sitting at one end of the oval cherry table, sipping coffee as he perused the morning paper, the evidence of his completed meal lying to one side.

"You were sleeping so soundly, kitten, that I went ahead and fixed myself some breakfast," Bob said as he saw his daughter come in.

"I'm surprised I slept so late. I usually don't."

"Well, now, after the excitement last night, it's understandable. Did you have a good time?" he inquired with a benevolent smile.

Skirting the issue of the announcement, Stacy answered, "Yes, after the party Drew took me to dine at a fabulous French restaurant. The food was out of this world."

"Glad you enjoyed yourself. Drew's a fine man; he'll make a good husband."

"Yes." Stacy hoped he did not take note of her blunt response. Their relationship was so close that she hated the idea of his disappointment when the engagement ended. Again, she wished that her life would get back to normal quickly and then she could stop feeling guilty about this web of deceit. Trying to keep her voice natural, she told him, "Oh, by the way, Drew is planning to take me out this afternoon."

"That's fine. I'll be busy with some work that piled up while we were away." With that, he folded the paper and dropped it on the table as he pushed back his chair. He walked over to his daughter and kissed her lightly on the cheek. "Have fun this afternoon."

"Thanks, Dad." She had not missed his sluggish movements and added, "Please don't keep at it too long today. Remember, it's Saturday; you should take it easy."

"Yes, kitten, later. But this morning I intend to clear up my backlog."

Stacy wisely said no more as he left the room, knowing that at this point it would only irritate him. From past experience she knew he would not relax until his work was done.

Carrying his dirty dishes to the sink, she rinsed them off, and, with a glance at the wall clock, she realized there was not enough time for a second meal before Drew arrived, so she decided to fix herself a substantial breakfast. The room was papered in a bright pattern and the harvest-gold appliances added to the cheeriness. She enjoyed working in this kitchen, fitted with all the modern conveniences and adequate counter space. She fried eggs and bacon, and, adding toast, juice, and coffee, ate at the place she set at the breakfast counter.

When she was finished, she restored the kitchen to order and then returned to her room to dress.

After a refreshing shower, she briskly dried herself with a soft terry towel; then she applied a light film of makeup and brushed out her glossy hair. Adhering to Drew's recommendation, she chose denim pants and jacket and with it a red T-shirt. The clothes hugged her trim figure, the pants accentuating her long legs.

Once dressed, Stacy wandered through the apartment putting things away and generally straightening up. In the living room she plumped up the pillows on the green and yellow quilted print sofa and deep green plush chairs. On the end table she found Drew's used glass and took it to the kitchen to put it in the dishwasher. Even while occupied with her chores, she could not blot out the memory of the preceding evening and the man who had kissed her so passionately. She could not work out a reasonable explanation for her uninhibited response. She deplored his type of man, who used women as playthings to be enjoyed for the moment and then casually tossed aside when another came along. She was just another in a long line; she had displaced Jennifer, and in a few weeks someone else would take her place. And yet—his touch stirred in her deeper feelings than any of the other men she had ever dated. Finally, she concluded that the only way to protect herself was to accept the current circumstances and not allow her emotions to get the better of her.

Filled with good intentions, Stacy calmly answered the doorbell when it chimed at the appointed hour. All of her clear-headed resolutions died when she looked up into his smoky-blue eyes with their potent magic.

"Hello, Stacy. All set?"

"Just about. Where are we going? I should let Dad know." She was relieved to discover she could speak so normally when all the time her composure was being strained by her unintentional response to his sexual appeal. He was dressed in Levi's™ which molded to his muscular thighs; tied loosely over his shoulders was a pullover sweater. The sleeves hung down his chest, but did not completely conceal the brown chest, with its mat of curly hairs exposed by his open-necked navy sport shirt. Her nose recognized the elusive scent of his after-shave.

"He knows where we'll be."

"He does? How?"

His mouth curled up in a smile. "I called earlier while you were still lazing around in bed."

Her hard-sought self-possession deserted her as his comment evoked a mental image. They had returned so late the night before that she had not bothered to find her nightgown and had slipped into bed naked.

As if divining her thoughts, Drew smiled knowingly. To conceal her embarrassment, Stacy suggested that they leave.

"Don't you want to say good-bye to your father?"

"Since he knows where I'll be, I won't disturb him."

When they reached Drew's car, which was parked at the foot of the steps, Stacy reached out for the door handle, but before she could open it, Drew's hand closed over hers.

"Allow me." Stung by his touch, she jumped back. The corner of his mouth lifted and she deliberately ignored his extended hand and climbed into the car.

As he headed out of the parking lot toward the main street, Stacy, determined to behave sensibly, said, "It's a beautiful day."

"Yes, it is," he responded briefly.

She searched her brain for a safe topic, and then, spotting the bumper-to-bumper line of cars, she said, "The traffic is pretty heavy."

"Usually is on Saturday afternoon." He slanted her a mocking smile.

Ooooh . . . he is so darned self-confident. He's doing it deliberately, like a cat playing with a mouse. And I'm the mouse! She sank back without saying another word, refusing to afford him further amusement.

Their progress was slow, but once they reached the throughway the pace picked up. Because Drew had to contend with the congested lanes of traffic and Stacy obstinately gave no more than a one- or two-word response to any of his comments, their conversation lagged.

Gradually, her annoyance faded in the joys of the spring day, and yielding to her innate common sense, she resolved to enjoy the afternoon.

After driving several miles, Drew turned off the highway and drove down a twisting street which eventually crossed a bridge spanning the Houston ship channel.

Through her window Stacy saw ships lining the docks. Behind a high metal fence the space was filled with railroad tracks, freight cars, trucks, and warehouses, a hive of activity.

Out of the corner of his eye, Drew perceived her interest. "Amazing, isn't it?"

"I've never seen so many ships!"

"You've never been here before?" His voice held an astonished note.

She answered honestly, though slightly chagrined. "No. I guess it's typical that people living in a place all their lives take it for granted and don't explore the sites right at their own back door."

He nodded his agreement. "During the week there is a boat ride for tourists that takes you through the channel. But I like watching from the public observation platform."

"Is that where we're headed?"

"Uh-huh. It's clear today so we'll have a terrific view." He stopped for a moment at a gate, explaining to the guard on duty where they were going. The older man waved them on and Drew drove down a gravel road, turned left, and parked between two station wagons.

As soon as Stacy alighted from the car she felt the strong breeze blowing in from the coast and carrying with it the salty scent of the sea along with the less pleasant smells of waste products created by man and machine.

Taking Stacy's hand in his own, Drew steered her across the wooden walkway leading to the observation platform which was built high above one end of the channel. Then they climbed up the first flight of steps single file so people descending could pass them. Sea gulls swooped above them sounding their raucous caws.

Drew's voice rose above the din created by the birds and wind. "Better view on the top. Keep going."

"Okay." But at the foot of the second set of stairs, Stacy paused to scan the scene below. "How can you tell where all these ships are from?"

Stopping behind her, Drew leaned one hand against the pine banister and looked out over Stacy's shoulder. "Each ship flies her country's flag. There's a chart with pictures of the flags and the countries they represent. Let's go on up and I'll show you."

She regarded the steep steps and grimaced.

"It's not that bad," Drew teased as he caught her expression. "You'll find the view worth the effort." He gave her a light push.

"Okay . . . okay. I'm going . . . I'm going." She trudged upward until she reached the flat planks forming the upper story, went to the railing, and leaned forward with her hands braced against the weathered beam. Drew followed and stood beside her.

From her vantage point she observed the wharves directly in front of the platform. A ship with a black hull was berthed a few hundred feet away in the murky water and she saw the crewmen cleaning her. Farther away a crane worked, lifting freight out of a ship's hold, and over to her right she noticed a wide, almost circular, body of water.

Raising a hand to point, she asked, "What's that?"

Drew traced the direction of her gesture with his eyes. "That is the ship basin. The channel is too narrow for most of the ships to turn around, so they head up here to make their U-turn."

Laughing, Stacy said, "I hope they don't have too many traffic jams. It would be a little difficult to get those ships untangled."

With a twinkle in his eyes, he responded, "That's why the port authority controls the traffic." He directed her attention eastward. "If you look out there you can see some of the ships waiting for a berth."

After watching silently for several more minutes, Drew took her arm and led her over to the flag chart.

"My gosh! I didn't know there were so many!"

"Houston is the third largest port in the United States, and ships sail here from all over the world. Some are too large for the Panama Canal, so they have to travel all the way around Cape Horn in South America. Those oil tankers can carry loads up to half a million tons. We've even had Russian ships tie up here to take on cargoes of grain." They strolled back to the railing, Stacy constantly aware of the man beside her, her skin sensitive to every casual touch.

"This is fascinating." She smiled up at Drew. "Thanks for bringing me."

"My pleasure." The look he gave her was so warm her breath caught in her throat and she swiftly turned back toward the channel.

She heard his voice continue: "I enjoy coming here. There's something mystical about watching ships."

"It's very exciting," Stacy murmured. Then in a stronger voice, she added, "Those men roam the oceans of the world, pitting themselves against the elements of nature."

"Right. Of course, it's not as dangerous as it was in the days of clipper ships or marauding pirates. Sailing ships have a certain aura, but life on them was harsh. If a ship was becalmed for several days, it could have resulted in starvation or dying of thirst."

"I guess you're right, but it must have been thrilling to watch the sails filled with wind, billowing like small white clouds."

"Would you have liked to live back then?" Drew asked as he saw the wistful expression in her eyes.

Stacy laughed lightly at her foolishness. "Not really. I enjoy living with the discoveries of modern science too much, although man does not seem able to cope with all of his technological advances."

"I understand. For instance, man has discovered cures for deadly diseases but can't eliminate smog."

Forcing her eyes away from this enigmatic man, Stacy swept back strands of hair from her eyes and gazed once more at the ships. She remembered reading somewhere that they could be as high as a ten-story building and as long as three football fields. From this distance, she could believe it!

"The wind seems to be getting stronger," observed Stacy, grasping her burnished locks at the nape of her neck to keep them from blowing around her face.

Drew agreed, smoothing back his own blond hair

with his fingers. It did not stay in place for more than the time it took him to do it.

"If you're ready we'll head for the car."

"Okay." Still holding her hair with one hand, she held the banister with the other. The steep descent was more precarious than the ascent. Just as she neared the bottom of the last flight, the gusting breeze blew tendrils of hair across her eyes. Momentarily blinded, her foot missed the next tread and though she tried to regain her balance, gripping onto the railing, the pull of gravity was too strong and she stumbled across the remaining steps, landing on her hands and knees.

In an instant, Drew was crouched at her side, his face bent close to hers. Even in her distress she felt his warm breath caress her cheek.

"Stacy! Are you all right?" She could only nod her head. Tears of pain and frustration blurred her eyes and choked her throat. As she struggled to her feet, his hands reached out, supporting her arms. Once she was standing he let go and dusted off her knees. She flinched.

"I must have grazed my knees." She checked her palms, and she was relieved to see that they were only red and puffy from the impact.

"She's all right, folks. If you'll let us pass I'll take her to the car." He spoke authoritatively to the cluster of curious onlookers. They moved aside, and Stacy began her painful progress, unable to avoid limping.

With a muttered oath, Drew picked her up in his arms. "Put your arms around my neck," he commanded. She obeyed, but her body was rigid. "Relax. It'll be easier on both of us."

"I'm sorry, but I'm not accustomed to this mode of transportation," she gulped before leaning her head on his woolly shoulder.

He chuckled. "You can't be hurt too badly if you're
making silly jokes."

"I can walk!"

"Sure you can—that's why you hobbled like a little
old lady."

"Oh, you!" She thumped his chest with her palm.
"You always have to be right. Male superiority and all
that!"

"Calm down. I could dump you in the water. That
would cool you off fast."

Stacy allowed herself an exaggerated sigh before
biting her tongue on another caustic remark. Then, as
he strode back down the walkway, she couldn't resist
exploring his sun-weathered features through the con-
cealment of her thick, dark lashes: the tan column of
his throat; the firmly clenched jaw; the sensual curve of
his mouth; the flaring nostrils; and the deep blue eyes
lightened by pinpoints of color. She assumed her
observations went undetected until she reached the
quirked eyebrows. Hastily, she shifted her glance away,
thankfully noting that his long strides had almost
carried them to the Corvette.

He set her down on the shining black hood and
unlocked the door. Stacy wriggled to the edge, preparing to stand up, when she heard Drew tell her, "Wait
where you are."

"I'm not helpless."

He glanced pointedly at her knees and raised a
mocking brow. "Oh, no? I have a first-aid kit in the car.
Do something useful. Roll up your pants."

Stacy acquiesced, relieved that she was not wearing
pantyhose. Heaven knew what he would have demanded then!

He levered himself into the car and found the small
box marked with a bright red cross. Setting it next to
her, he inspected her knees. "You're lucky your slacks

protected you. You'll have bruises on both knees, but the skin's only broken on one."

"I'm glad the mini-skirt isn't in style."

"Oh, but you have such great legs." He ran his fingers lightly over her calf muscle, triggering impulses up her nerves. She stiffened.

"Hurry up! People are staring." Her haughty voice disguised her agitation.

"Let them. It doesn't bother me." He finished treating her grazed knee and she quickly unrolled her pants legs. Then, as she began to slide off the hood, he scooped her up and deposited her on the leather cushion.

"Stretch out your legs," he ordered. "That way they won't stiffen up."

"Yes, sir," she returned demurely.

He cast her a swift glance, sensing her mild tone held more to it.

Delighted in seeing him somewhat baffled, Stacy was unprepared for his gentle kiss. Then he explained, "That's for being a 'good' little girl."

Her eyes round with surprise, all she could utter was a soft exclamation. If he heard her, he took no notice as he folded his long frame into the car and replaced the first-aid box under her seat, his arm brushing her thigh. Flustered by this further contact, Stacy looked steadily out the window, mentally reciting the alphabet in an effort to suppress her inflamed senses.

When they were on the road, Drew asked, "Should I take you straight home, or would you care to join me for an early dinner?"

"I'd like to have dinner," answered Stacy, unable to resist his invitation. Rationally, she knew it would be better not to spend too much time in Drew's company, but found she could not behave wisely in his presence.

"Good. I'm hungry."

Before long he was pulling up before an unimpressive downtown restaurant. "How are your legs?" he asked, switching off the engine.

"I can walk," she told him. During the drive she had flexed her legs several times as the pain subsided and now felt perfectly capable of managing the short distance from the curb to the entrance.

She read the sign. "I've never been here before."

"Get ready for pure delight. I discovered this place during my college days when money was tight. Señora Garcia never lets anyone leave hungry."

Once Stacy's eyes adjusted to the dimly lit room, she saw a large Mexican-American woman approaching. With an enthusiastic hug for Drew, she said, "Drew Pitman! It's so good to see you! Where have you been keeping yourself?"

He returned her embrace. "Señora, you remember me!"

"It hasn't been that long, nor am I so old that I wouldn't remember a man who ate so many of my tamales." The *señora* glanced at both of their lean figures. "Come, I need to fatten you up."

They both chuckled. Then Drew raised Stacy's left hand as he introduced her to the older woman. "Señora Garcia, this is my fiancée, Señorita Davidson."

"Oh, ho. So you are to be married." Her face was wreathed in smiles. "That is nice. Come, come." She gestured them to leather chairs set at a heavy wooden table next to the far wall. Beautifully woven rugs decorated the plaster walls. "You have come early. I have not too many customers right now. I will serve you myself. What would you like?"

"We'll start with *nachos,* and then how 'bout some enchiladas and *refritos.*" He glanced at Stacy, who indicated her agreement. "And we'll both take a beer."

"Of course. Anything else? No tamales?"

Before Drew could answer, Stacy spoke up. "Stop, please. That's enough. I want to be able to walk away from the table!" she chided laughingly.

"Just wait until you taste the *señora's* food. You will not be able to resist eating everything in sight." The *señora* hurried off to the kitchen, her face beaming from Drew's praise.

He looked after the woman fondly. Then, resting his elbows on the table, he turned his attention to Stacy, who said, "She's very nice."

"Yes, she is," he agreed. "She treats everyone like that. Her daughters and even some of her grandchildren work for her."

"A real family business."

His eyes took on a distant expression, his mouth a grim line. Señora Garcia brought the nachos and beer. Drew mumbled his thanks and she left, saying, "The rest of your dinner will be ready soon."

Perceiving by his remoteness that something was amiss, Stacy said, "You've never told me—do you have a large family?"

"What . . .? Oh . . . no. Just my mother's left. Dad died when I was in grade school."

"No brothers or sisters?" she probed.

"No . . . my mother had a miscarriage three years after I was born, and she was told then that she would never have any others."

Stacy sensed a common bond; they were both only children, forever missing the closeness of a brother or sister. But she had been lucky. She had a good relationship with her father and, before she had died, with her mother.

"That's too bad," she said aloud, her voice deep with inexpressible sympathy.

"It was soon after that when my mother took up painting. It seemed to fill the void in her life," he said baldly, his voice devoid of any emotion, but the muscles of his face had tightened.

"What about you?" She sat with her hands clasped on the table in front of her.

"She was always around, but I was an independent kid. There were neighborhood children to play with and it wasn't long before I started school."

Stacy yearned to reach out to this formidable man who had built a wall around his inner soul. In her mind's eye she saw a lonely little boy, fiercely proud.

Rousing himself, Drew sank back in his chair, a corner of his mouth lifted self-derisively. "Enough of my childhood. Here comes our dinner. And from the smell of it, I'd say Señora Garcia has outdone herself."

One by one the *señora* set out plates and bowls. "Enjoy! It is my pleasure," she told them.

They ate slowly, savoring the hot spicy food and the cool brew which eased their burning mouths. Conversation was centered around their feast. Finally, with a groan, Stacy protested as Drew offered her more. "No!" She put out her hand to stop his.

Chuckling, he looked down at her restraining fingers and, self-consciously, she jerked them back. Meanwhile, he was saying smoothly, "All right. You needn't eat anymore." He rubbed a hand across his taut mid-section. "I'd better quit, too."

Minutes later, with warm words of affection ringing in their ears, Drew took her home.

Hesitating in front of her door, Stacy asked, "Do you have time to come in?"

"Sure. It's still early."

They found Bob in the living room, still going over business papers. His daughter regarded him reproachfully. "I thought you were going to take it easy today."

Bob glanced ruefully at the incriminating evidence.

"I went for a walk this afternoon." He put the papers with some others on a side table and went to his daughter, sliding his arm around her shoulders. "Don't fuss . . . I'm done for the day." With a glance in Drew's direction, he changed the subject by asking, "Can I offer you something to drink?"

"I'll have a beer. My mouth is still burning from our Mexican dinner."

Before Bob could move, Stacy had ducked out from under his arm and headed for the kitchen, calling back over her shoulder. "I'll get it. Same for you, Dad?" He nodded his head in agreement and then motioned Drew over to an easy chair. "Come sit down."

When Stacy returned with a Lucite™ tray loaded with frosty beer mugs and a soda for herself, the men were seated, discussing business matters. After serving them, she set the tray on the coffee table and relaxed against the sofa cushions, slowly sipping her drink, the bubbles of carbonation tickling the roof of her mouth and quenching her thirst.

Several minutes passed and Drew sent her an inquiring glance. Puzzled, she looked back at him, her brow wrinkling in a frown.

"Are we boring you?" he asked.

"Not at all."

But her father checked his watch. "My, look at the time." He paused to stretch and stifled an obvious yawn. "If you'll excuse me, I'll be saying good night." Bob kissed his daughter on the forehead and with a twinkle in his eye reminded her not to stay up too late.

As his retreating form disappeared down the hallway, Drew moved next to Stacy, his arm resting across the sofa back.

"Your father is a very understanding man." His tone held a hint of laughter.

"He probably thought we'd like to be . . . alone." Stacy floundered over the last word. *Why is it*, she wondered, *that as soon as he's close to me I lose my head? I'm not a teen-ager, flustered by the mere presence of the opposite sex.*

Drew's knee nudged her thigh. She looked up, caught in his spell as he moved in closer. "Thoughtful of him."

She was disturbed by his actions, but before she could evade him, he possessed her lips, leaning his weight against her sensitive breasts, pinning her against the sofa, capturing her between his arms. Her first reaction was to resist, her hands pushing ineffectively against his shoulders, but his touch destroyed her defenses, igniting something deep within her soul, and she responded to her natural needs, giving him back kiss for kiss. Drew paused momentarily to look into her eyes and Stacy felt mesmerized by his smoldering gaze; he murmured softly, his lips gently caressing her cheek, and then they traveled down to the hollow of her throat. Her heart pounded against his chest. All coherent thoughts were wiped away, all resistance gone when she slid her arms around his neck, her fingers twining in his hair just as he moved to invade her throbbing mouth once more with his own.

He released her, shifted his body away. "It's time for me to go," he said briefly, somewhat breathless.

Stacy straightened up and watched as he sprang to his feet and moved toward the hallway, reminded indefinably of a strutting rooster.

"Good night, Stacy—I'll phone you soon." His words rang in her ears . . . a sop to her self-respect.

Resentful, she wanted to chastise him for exploiting his status as her fiancé, but when she found her voice the front door was closed. Drew was gone. She smashed her curled fingers down into a pillow, frustrated with him . . . but, most of all, with herself.

Disconsolate, she pushed herself up, switched off the lights, and crept off to her room.

Chapter Five

The golden glow from sunbeams sparkling through the panes of stained glass and reflecting off the mosaic-tiled wall illuminated the church with a radiant light.

Stacy felt an upsurge of strength and energy as her tensions and concerns for the future eased under the calming influence of this holy place. She had not slept well the night before and had awakened early, feeling dispirited and listless. After breakfast, her father had assumed that they were going to follow their usual Sunday morning routine and Stacy could not disappoint him. So she had changed into a long-sleeved russet dress and had accompanied him to church, although she only wanted to crawl back under the covers and try to sink into the forgetfulness of sleep. During the early morning hours she had been plagued with dreams of Drew Pitman. No matter how hard she tried to remain aloof, her resistance was destroyed each time he touched her.

She had dated a number of men through the years, but she had never behaved so wantonly. After a good-night kiss, she would send them on their way, and anyone who tried to cajole her into further intimacies or argue with her old-fashioned standards would be told off without a twinge of regret. But with Drew she was no longer in control, and it frightened her. He was an experienced man who did not fall into one of her neat little categories, and she felt as though she had gotten in way beyond her depth. All she could hope for was an early conclusion of their engagement so she could end this torment.

Around and around in her mind it went; until now, in the peace of the church, she had found an inner strength to temporarily still her mental conflict.

After the minister gave the benediction, Stacy smiled up at her father and he took her arm as they made their way out to the narthex. There they visited with several friends, Stacy secure in her father's loving care.

Through the crowd she suddenly spied Katie and her mother, Muriel Goodwin, and with a whispered explanation to Bob they headed in their direction, pausing only briefly to greet more people.

The older woman had dressed in a powder blue suit which flattered her attractively styled greying brown hair. Her features were a matured version of her daughter's, who wore a navy dress with scarlet piping around the collar, cuffs, and waistline.

"Bob and Stacy, how nice to see you." Mrs. Goodwin graciously offered her hand to Bob Davidson and he clasped it warmly, enfolding it in both of his.

"Muriel, we haven't seen you in ages. How are you?" His words were simple enough but his message carried a deeper meaning since they had met only rarely since her husband's funeral the year before.

"I'm doing just fine. My daughter here persuaded me

to come to the early service. I usually wait until the later one; it's not so crowded."

"I, for one, am glad you did." There was a sparkle in his eye.

"Thank you." She sounded inordinately pleased.

While they were speaking, the two girls had been conversing between themselves, but their attention was brought back to their parents as Muriel said, "Why don't you and Stacy join us for dinner?"

"Oh, we couldn't impose on you like that," Bob protested halfheartedly.

"It's no imposition at all," Katie spoke up enthusiastically. "Mom insisted on making a roast today, and there is more than enough for all of us."

"It sounds like a good idea, Dad," Stacy said, adding her vote to the proposal.

Bob spoke. "Well, how can I resist three delightful ladies?"

The rest of the conversation focused on arrangements for driving their separate cars and meeting at the Goodwins' home, which was located a couple of miles from the church.

Not too many minutes later they had all regathered in the Goodwins' living room. It was a large room but decorated with warm, colorful fabrics, giving it a homey atmosphere. The succulent aromas drifting in from the kitchen offered enticing testimony to Muriel's earlier preparations. For a while they all joined in on a lively discussion of current events. Then Muriel broke in to excuse herself.

Before she could rise to her feet, she was forestalled by her daughter's thoughtful command. "Mom, you sit and enjoy our guests. I think I can manage things in the kitchen."

"Why, thank you, dear." Her eyes crinkled as she smiled fondly at her only daughter.

"I'll help her," Stacy offered, jumping to her feet and refusing to be swayed by Katie's protests. "Two can work much faster than one," she pointed out logically.

While she washed her hands at the kitchen sink, Katie spied Stacy's engagement ring. "My gosh, Stacy, what a beautiful ring!" exclaimed her excited friend, grasping her left hand. "When did you get it?"

"Friday night," was all she gave by way of an answer, wary of the thoughtful reflection in Katie's eyes.

"Oh . . . so Drew Pitman's the lucky man," she guessed shrewdly. "Why did you keep it a secret?" A troubled frown creased her forehead.

Stacy had deliberately kept her left hand out of sight earlier, fearing her friend's curiosity and unrealistically hoping that she would not have to make any explanations. "He surprised me," she said, trying to stick as close to the truth as possible. "Believe me, I had no idea." Fortunately, Katie did not recognize the note of sarcasm.

"Boy, what a surprise!" She considered her friend suspiciously. "You don't sound too pleased."

Stacy managed a light chuckle and smiled brightly, but it didn't quite reach her brown eyes, as she responded, "Of course I am. Drew's a wonderful man."

She must have sounded convincing, for, after a brief hesitation, the other girl said, "Aren't you lucky! Am I going to have a chance to meet him?"

"Probably," Stacy hedged, thinking wildly of the bottomless pit of lies she was falling into.

"When?" Katie persisted.

"I can't say definitely; Drew has such an erratic schedule." Katie's expression drooped and Stacy added, "But I'll try to make it as soon as possible."

"Just so it's before the wedding," Katie warned teasingly.

"Of course." Stacy suppressed a sign of relief as Katie was distracted by the hissing of a pot boiling over on the stove. After the burner's knob was turned down, she asked, "What can I do to help?"

Katie put down the fork she was using to test the vegetables and nodded in the direction of the dining room. "Why don't you sent the table? Do you know where everything is?"

"Yes, unless your mother has moved things around."

"Not a chance." She sounded amused. "Nothing in this house has been moved in years except for cleaning."

"This is kind of like old times. Remember when we used to visit each other practically every day?" she said, thinking fondly of those carefree days.

Katie added sentimentally, her eyes lit with a distant gleam, "Yes, those were good times." Her words reminded Stacy that during the intervening years since high school they had both suffered the loss of one parent.

"Well, enough chitchat. This isn't getting dinner on the table." Stacy forced out a light laugh which broke the gloomy spell.

Katie's face relaxed. "So . . . get movin'!"

Stacy went through the swing door to the dining room. In the large, cherry china cabinet she found place mats, silver, china, and glasses. She quickly set out four plates around the oval table.

From across the hallway she could hear the voluble voices of the remaining occupants of the living room. Smiling smugly to herself, she filled the glasses from a pitcher of ice water, pleased with the success of her little maneuvers. Her father's work consumed most of his days, and she knew he needed more time off, spent with friends with whom he had common interests. As far as she was concerned, Muriel Goodwin fit the bill perfectly, and from the sound of their voices they had discovered the same thing.

Katie stuck her head through the door. "Stacy, would you go tell our parents it's time to eat?"

"Okay." She nodded in the direction of the living room and queried amusedly, "They seem to be having a good time. Are you sure we should break it up?"

"Yes, if we don't want to eat a dried-out roast," Katie returned wryly.

"I'm on my way." She pivoted on her heel and walked to the living room, pausing just inside the doorway. Her father, now without his suit coat, was sitting at one end of the sofa, his arm stretched across the back, while he used the other to emphasize a point to Muriel, who was listening attentively from the other corner of the sofa.

Only by clearing her throat discreetly did Stacy gain their attention. "Dinner is ready."

"Oh, my. I didn't realize how long we had been talking," Muriel offered, her eyes wide with surprise. "You should have called me."

"No need for that; Katie had everything well under control," Stacy told her soothingly. "Besides, I'm sure Dad was glad you stayed to entertain him." She twinkled over at her father.

"That's right," he agreed, then stood up. With a gallant gesture, he offered his arm to Muriel, and when they reached the table, he courteously seated her.

"It looks like you girls thought of everything," Muriel said as she surveyed the steaming serving dishes piled high with mashed potatoes and broccoli, the mesh basket of rolls, and the gravy boat.

"All but the roast," Katie announced, carrying in

said item. She said to Bob, "Would you do the honors?"

"My pleasure." Katie set the platter in front of Bob, who rubbed his hands together. "Perfect." He picked up the carving knife and fork and set to work. After carefully slicing several thin pieces, he said at random, "Glad I haven't lost the knack."

Stacy could not speak, overcome by memories of other Sunday dinners when her mother was still with them. Light chatter covered her silence until she recalled herself to the present as the dishes were passed around the table.

The rest of the dinner conversation revolved around a variety of topics until dessert, when Bob declared with a wistful note, "This has been nice." The others looked at him as he continued: "Stacy knows what I mean." He patted her hand which was resting next to his on the table. "Living in an apartment is convenient, but when we sold the house after Ellen died we lost that homey stability."

As she gave his hand a squeeze and smiled reassuringly, Stacy discovered she was on the verge of tears.

Muriel spoke up. "I've often wondered whether I should consider selling this place." She cast her eyes around the room. "But I've never quite been able to do it."

"Then don't," Bob told her firmly. "You're happy here—unless, of course, it's financially impossible." Their long-established friendship made his words inoffensive.

"No . . . no. I was very lucky. Our savings have been invested wisely."

"That's good." His voice sounded relieved. "Your situation is completely different from ours. With both of us working and traveling, we decided it would be best to live in a much smaller place." He paused to gaze fondly at his daughter. "Now that Stacy's on the brink of marriage, I'm glad I won't be rattling around in some big, old house."

When Muriel expressed no surprise at his comment, Stacy assumed that it had been discussed earlier, and Muriel's next remark confirmed it.

"I've been meaning to offer you my best wishes, Stacy."

"Thank you," Stacy murmured, her guilt tightening her throat.

"I've heard of Drew Pitman, but I've never met him personally."

"Haven't we all," Katie added teasingly, a little imp of mischief sparkling in her eyes. "I've made Stacy promise that I'll have a chance to meet him before the wedding. Who knows, maybe he'll fall for my fatal charm."

"Too late for that, 'dearest friend,'" Stacy quipped back.

"Ah, well, better luck next time." The light banter continued off and on for the rest of the afternoon. By the time they were preparing to leave, Stacy was worn out with her efforts to sustain the illusion of a happily engaged woman.

At last they were being shown to the door, thanking their friends for such a pleasant afternoon.

"We've enjoyed it thoroughly," Muriel was quick to respond as she held out her hand to Bob. He grasped it firmly, holding it just a shade longer than necessary.

"Thanks again . . . bye . . . for now." His voice was low.

"Bye, Bob . . . and you take care of your dad, Stacy," she charged the young woman and chuckled as the man groaned.

"I'm not completely helpless."

"Of course you're not," she told him, but at the same time she gave his daughter a knowing wink. Stacy grinned conspiratorially.

The following morning, bright and early, Stacy dressed in a moss-green skirt and matching jacket which flattered the copper highlights in her hair, now twisted into a bun, and set off proudly with her father for work. He wore a dark business suit for the office, unlike the work clothes he used out at the sites.

The office building was only two short blocks away, and they preferred to walk and thus have some time together before they were caught up in the hectic pace of their working roles.

The brisk morning air was invigorating. The sun, still low in the eastern sky, held the promise of yet another glorious day. The trees with their new mantle of green and the dew sparkling off the grass buoyed Stacy's flagging spirits and added a bounce to her steps. She had not heard from Drew since Saturday night, and she was exasperated with herself for minding so much. Every time their phone rang her pulse had automatically accelerated and she had reached for it eagerly, only to be disappointed time and again.

Her youthful spirit could not stay low for long, though, with this burgeoning display of nature all around. Words alone could not express her feelings, but she knew instinctively that her father felt the same way, for she had trouble keeping up with his long strides, and the tight lines on his face had eased a fraction.

Once in the office, Stacy filled the automatic coffee maker set in one corner of her office. Then she went to her desk to sort through the mail. The furnishings were geared for efficiency, but the brown laminated file drawers, linen drapes, tweed carpet, and upholstered chairs softened the functional atmosphere.

Armed with mugs of steaming coffee and her steno pad tucked under one arm, Stacy walked into the opulent inner office. She placed one cup within her father's reach before seating herself in a chair opposite him. With only an occasional hasty sip of her own coffee, she efficiently took the dictation for several letters and then awaited further instructions.

"I'll have my report ready to type once those letters are done."

She leafed through the pages of shorthand. "These should take about an hour."

"Perfect. All that work of mine over the weekend paid off," he admitted with a wry twist to his lips.

"Well, then, you can slow down a little today . . . hmm?"

He regarded the assorted papers on his desk. "Not today. Now that the report's done, I have another project to work on."

His daughter gave a disgruntled sigh.

"You can be replaced," he said with mock reproof.

"Yes, sir." Stacy sketched him a salute and danced out of the office, gently closing the door behind her.

After typing several pages, the sound of an opening door caused her to pause with her fingers on the keys as Paul Elmwood entered the office.

"Morning, Stacy. Can the boss see me?"

"Hi, Paul. I'll check." She lifted the receiver and dialed the inter-office number. After speaking briefly, she told Paul that he could go right in.

"Thanks. Will you be here later?"

She spread her hands in a comprehensive gesture over the loaded desk and said with a twinkle, "That's highly probable."

"Good. I want to talk to you."

She pointed out, "You're keeping him waiting."

With a quick tap on the door, he entered the district superintendent's office.

Stacy kept up her swift attack on the typewriter keys until Paul came back and stood beside her desk. Politely she gave him her attention. She saw him study her left hand, an odd expression flitting across his face, before he asked, "Stacy, can I take you to lunch?"

The phone rang and, murmuring a brief apology, she answered it. Instantly, her complete concentration was riveted to the instrument as she recognized the caller's voice. "Drew!" she exclaimed softly, her heart missing a beat.

"Right on the first try," he teased.

"How are you?" she asked in a cooler voice.

"Just fine. I called to let you know I'd be out of town for several days."

"Thanks for calling." Her tone had become stiff as she tried to control an overwhelming surge of melancholy.

His voice continued mockingly: "I didn't want you thinking I was neglecting you." He paused and then said in such a way that she almost could believe he meant it sincerely, "Think about me while I'm away. . . . Bye."

"Good-bye, Drew . . . take care." The last words were said an instant before the line went dead. Slowly she replaced the receiver, a mental image of Drew's rugged features clouding her vision.

Paul's disgruntled voice dispelled her abstraction. "So that was the absent fiancé?"

"Yes," was her terse reply. She kept her eyes shadowed with her long, thick lashes.

"Does that mean you're tied up for lunch?"

"No. On the contrary, he called to say he was going out of town."

"Good." There was a self-satisfied note to his voice. "Then you can have lunch with me?" he pressured.

"I don't know," she hedged. "A friend of mine is going to be here this morning to apply for a job. She may be expecting me to have lunch with her."

"Can't you put her off?" he asked petulantly.

"What's the big deal?" Instantly, she was ashamed at the harsh tone of her voice. She saw that he seemed ill at ease, his right hand fiddling with the knot of his tie.

He looked pointedly at her left hand and then up to her sable-brown eyes. "I'd like to talk with you privately."

Drew's earlier assessment of Paul's affection flashed through her mind and she intuitively guessed that he wanted to discuss her engagement. In a last-ditch effort to avoid a drawn-out interrogation, she asked, "Can't you talk to me now?" With a slight wave of her hand, she indicated the empty office.

"No . . . we could be interrupted. It would be better over lunch."

Reluctantly, she decided that it would be more expedient for the office routine if they got this "private" chat over with today. She took a deep breath.

"I haven't made any definite plans with Katie, so I guess I can go."

He seemed relieved. "One o'clock?"

"Okay."

"See you later."

She muttered under her breath, but he did not notice her less-than-enthusiastic response since he was already out the door. She resumed typing, refusing to speculate on his motive until her suspicions were definitely confirmed. She comforted herself with the idea that just possibly he wanted to talk about his work, or something to do with business.

The rest of the morning flew by. Once the letters were typed, signed, and in the mail, she started the lengthy report, her progress occasionally interrupted by business calls and visitors, but no Katie Goodwin.

When Paul came to pick her up, Stacy was nearing the bottom of the page, so she indicated a chair and asked him to wait until she finished. With his elbow propped on the arm of the chair, he supported his chin in his hand while beating an impatient tattoo on the arm with the other. The irksome noise strained Stacy's nerves and it took longer than normal to finish. Once she pulled the sheet from the machine, his tapping ceased and he stood hovering near the doorway while she added it to the stack and locked them away in a file drawer.

"Ready?" he harried her.

"Just a second," she returned evenly, somehow able to suppress her irritation. "I'll let Dad know I'm leaving and then we can go." After she informed her father, she opened a drawer, grasped her purse, pushed back her chair, and rose to her feet.

As they walked down the hall, Stacy suggested blandly, but with a mischievous flicker of her eyes, "Do you mind if we use the stairs? It's only three flights, and I need the exercise after sitting at that desk all morning."

Disgruntled, Paul agreed. When they reached the bottom of the stairwell, he said, slightly breathless from his exertion, "I'm ready to sit. You may not have done much moving around today, but I have."

Impervious to his reproof, she continued on to the lunchroom, which was situated in the building's ground level. When she reached the entrance she paused and

searched the crowded room for a vacant table. She
spotted one over in one corner and, touching Paul on
his jacket sleeve, led the way. A harassed young
waitress brought glasses of water and two menus, but
Paul waved them aside.

"We don't have much time, so just give me the club
sandwich on whole wheat." Then he regarded his
companion inquiringly.

She had not known of any need for haste, but she
quickly decided to order a bowl of vegetable soup.

When they were alone, Stacy asked, "Why the
rush?"

"I don't want to waste time. You never know how
long it will take her to return."

Stacy could think of nothing to say, so she sipped her
ice water and waited for Paul to begin. She noticed his
eyes were fixed once more on her ring. Any hopes for a
business discussion were banished, and she did not
anticipate his quizzing with pleasure.

After a moment he looked up, the muscles of his face
tight. "I see you have an engagement ring. . . . When
did you get it?"

"Drew gave it to me Friday night."

"Stacy, I thought we were friends . . . good friends."
He emphasized the last two words.

"We are, Paul . . . I like working with you."

"That's all?" He sounded nettled, his brown eyes
pools of reproach.

What can I say? she wondered desperately. She did
not want to hurt him, but she knew that even without
her engagement to Drew there would never be anything more than friendship between them; the few
kisses they had shared had never sparked off the
tumultuous feelings that Drew's kisses inspired.

Aloud, she said as gently as she could, "I'm sorry,
Paul. I consider you a dear friend." Her eyes dropped

and she stared at a point on his left shoulder. "I'm very happy to be engaged to Drew."

"I had the impression that you enjoyed going out with me."

Her conscience smote her, but she forced herself to discourage his hopes once and for all. Looking him straight in the eye, she said, "We've had some good times together, Paul, but I'm in love with Drew."

He scrutinized her intently and after a moment he said, "I guess there's nothing left for me to say." His shoulders slumped.

She was aware of his dejection, but she could only sit silently, mentally chastising herself for the pain she had inflicted.

Fortunately, at that point they were distracted by the waitress. After they were served she asked, "Anything else?"

"No, thanks. Everything's fine," Stacy answered for them both.

As they ate, Stacy's mind shifted unavoidably to her declaration. Could it be true? Could she be in love with Drew Pitman? Was that what lent such conviction to her words? Of all people! His only interest in women was to use them to satisfy his own animal needs. *No!* She would not become prey to his overpowering charm!

Paul's puzzled voice intruded and Stacy stared at him blankly for a moment before her vision cleared and she recalled herself to the moment.

"I didn't realize you had known Drew Pitman." He continued as if trying to sort through some facts which did not add up. "Why didn't you mention it when he was called in?"

She avoided answering by biting into a cracker. At last she swallowed and said firmly, "We've already explained everything to my father's satisfaction."

"It just doesn't add up."

Now she was annoyed. It was not really any of his business! Why was he being such a bore by pursuing these questions? Lowering her spoon, she glared at him and answered with a hint of impatience, "It isn't any of your concern, so quit cross-examining me."

"Sorry, but as your friend I think I have the right." He drew back his shoulders and puffed out his chest.

"Thanks, but I can take care of myself."

"Can you?" His voice was dubious.

"Yes, I can," she asserted more firmly than she felt. Then, casting her eyes away from his mournful gaze, she glimpsed Katie standing by the doorway. Glad for an excuse to terminate his inquisition, she stood up and signaled her friend. "There's Katie," she explained to Paul.

He grunted in response, but his attitude was mollified when she pleaded, "Please, Paul, be nice. She's had a rough time of it lately."

"Haven't we all," he muttered bitterly. "Okay, as a favor to you."

When Katie reached the table, Stacy made the necessary introductions.

She responded brightly to Paul's greeting. Then, unable to contain her news, she burst out, "I got the job!"

"That's terrific." Stacy hugged her friend and then admitted apologetically, "I'm sorry I don't have more time to celebrate right now, but I've got to finish typing an important report."

"That's okay. I understand." Some of her exuberance disappeared.

"Why don't you join me? I need another cup of coffee. How 'bout you?" Paul offered absently.

"I'd love one. Thank you." The sparkle returned to Katie's eyes, and without further prompting she seated herself in Stacy's empty chair.

"See you around, Paul," Stacy said, to which he barely nodded. And then Stacy said to Katie, "I'm glad we'll be seeing more of each other. Let's plan on having lunch together next week."

"I'd like that."

"Bye for now." Stacy sketched a wave as she hurried out, relieved to escape from Paul's probing.

Chapter Six

Slumping back in one of the living room chairs, Stacy watched the evening news. Suddenly, she leaned forward, her hands clutching the velvet armrest, her attention riveted as camera footage of an oil fire flashed on the screen. The commentator tersely outlined the details: "Yesterday morning an explosion occurred in a field southwest of Houston when a farm worker plowed through high weeds concealing a two-and-a-half-foot-high well head. The leaking gas ignited instantly, killing the driver. Drew Pitman was called in, and late this afternoon he has announced the fire is under control. There were no other serious injuries. . . ."

As the newsman droned on to the next story, Stacy heaved a sigh of relief and sank back, clenching her hands together to control their trembling.

"Looks like Drew was successful."

"Hmm?" Stacy twisted around in surprise and saw

her father standing just behind her chair. "Oh . . . yes
. . . everything's under control."

"He's a man you can sure be proud of."

Rising to her feet, she hesitated with her answer, but
as Bob waited expectantly, she said, "He sure is." She
considered him wisely. "You'd have enjoyed having a
son like him."

It was more a statement than a question, and Bob
responded, "Any man would, but I'll settle for him
being my son-in-law."

"How lucky can you get?" she said flippantly, her
mouth forced into a grin. Then she rushed on: "Dinner
will be in half an hour."

"Take your time."

Stacy walked swiftly to the kitchen and busied herself
with the meal's preparations. Gradually, her heart
resumed a steadier pace, but her mind could not blot
out the image of Drew as he had faced the television
camera. Even soot and grime had not camouflaged his
virile good looks and those smoky blue eyes had given
her the uncanny impression that he was looking straight
at her.

The next several days passed slowly. Although
secretarial duties filled her days, once the kitchen was
cleaned up from dinner Stacy found that the hours
dragged on until it was time for bed.

She arranged to have lunch with Katie at the end of
the week, but on Friday morning her friend called to
cancel. Deciding that she needed a break from the
office, Stacy left the building alone and set out for a
nearby café.

The past couple of days had been rainy and overcast,
matching her low spirits; luckily today the gloomy
clouds had disappeared and she walked leisurely,
reveling in the noonday sun, warm breeze, and fresh

earth scents. Auto traffic was heavy, but even its
cacophony did not disturb her buoyant spirits.

As she strolled down the sidewalk she noticed a tall
blond man in the crowd ahead. "He looks just like
Drew," she mused aloud, instantly perturbed by her
overactive imagination. Then, as the pedestrians
paused at the corner traffic light, the man in question
turned his head.

It *was* Drew!

Her brain registered her astonishment, but she was
unprepared for the lightning shot of pain she felt as she
glimpsed a woman's head resting intimately against his
shoulder. Instantly she recognized the unforgettable
blonde hair of Jennifer Hyatt!

Stunned, Stacy stopped dead, thus causing the man
behind her to ram into her. Embarrassed, she apologized to the stranger for her carelessness.

"That's all right. . . . Are you okay? You don't look
too good," said the pleasant young man, watching her
pale features uncertainly.

Forcing a smile to her lips, Stacy said, "I'm fine,
thank you. . . . I just remembered some work I need to
do."

"Any way I can help?"

This time her smile was warmer as she realized that
he was truly trying to lend his assistance.

"No, thank you."

"My fiancée will be fine." Unnoticed, Drew had
come up beside them. He glared at the innocuous
young man and, as if to confirm his rights, possessively
grasped Stacy by the elbow. Then he steered her
toward the corner as the baffled stranger shrugged his
shoulders and went briskly on his way.

"Was that necessary?" Stacy burst out, trying to
shake off his restraining hand.

"I think so."

"He was just being kind." Her eyes flashed.

"Oh, yeah?" he drawled. "You don't suppose it had anything to do with those big brown eyes of yours?"

Stacy held her tongue since they were now within earshot of Jennifer, who was waiting impatiently, tapping one elegantly shod foot.

Switching adroitly to an amiable tone, Drew said, "Darling, do you remember meeting Jennifer Hyatt at the Woodwards'?"

"Oh, yes," she responded with unnecessary sweetness. "There were many people there, but such a beautiful woman is unforgettable."

Drew scrutinized her briefly but Stacy had schooled her features into a credible smile.

The other woman's eyes flickered over her suspiciously as she murmured a polite rejoinder. Meanwhile, Stacy had difficulty restraining the impulse to say something more in keeping with her true attitude.

"Jennifer and I were just on our way to lunch. Care to join us?"

What colossal nerve! Stacy thought bitterly.

But before she could supply a scathing retort, Jennifer purred, "Yes, do come along."

Recognizing the condescension in her voice, Stacy's hackles rose.

"I'd be happy to," she told Jennifer with an innocent smile, but her eyes were glowing. "I'd like to get to know some of Drew's 'old friends.'"

The blonde woman's sharp intake of breath was proof enough for Stacy that her shot had hit home. Her slight smile was replaced by a silent cry of pain when Drew's fingers squeezed her flesh. Unrepentant, she tried to dig in her heels, but his superior strength propelled her across the intersection.

"The restaurant's not much farther. This must be my lucky day—two lovely companions for lunch."

Stacy could not see Jennifer's reaction as she clung to Drew's other arm, but his smugness incensed her further. Prudently, she bit her tongue on a sarcastic retort.

When they approached the entrance, Drew dropped their arms to swing open the door and gestured urbanely for them to precede him. Jennifer led the way into the softly lit foyer, which followed the motif of the early 1900s, with Tiffany-style lamps and polished wood floors. With Drew's commanding presence they were soon seated and their orders taken. Stacy and Drew opted for the beef stew, while Jennifer chose a salad, remarking that as a model she had to be careful of her weight.

Examining the thin figure clothed today in another blue dress, Stacy said, "Oh, I didn't realize you were a model."

"Yes. I've been featured in layouts for several of the big stores."

"How nice," Stacy returned in dulcet tones.

"I find the work very stimulating."

Stacy murmured another polite comment, noting out of the corner of her eyes by the upward tilt of his lips that Drew appeared faintly pleased about something. Then, giving Jennifer her undivided attention, she was inundated with highlights of the other woman's career.

Eventually, Drew switched the conversation to more general topics until Jennifer said, with a dramatic lift of her arched eyebrows, "You must tell me your secret, Stacy. How ever did you catch such an elusive bachelor?" Then her kitten-like gaze shifted to Drew.

Distrusting her effusive comment after her remarks at the party, Stacy said, with a touch of spirit, "You might say we fell into it." She smothered a giggle as Drew choked on a mouthful of food. "Oh, dear, are you all right?" She solicitously patted his back.

"Fine," he said tersely after sipping some water. With a strange glimmer in his eyes, he regarded Stacy and then told Jennifer, "My fiancée is too modest. I was trapped by her charms."

As he finished, his eyes went back to Stacy, whose cheeks brightened under his mocking scrutiny. She dropped her lashes.

As soon as she swallowed her last bite of stew, she excused herself on the pretext of needing to return to work.

"I'll see you out." Drew cut off her escape by swiftly rising to his feet and following her hasty steps to the foyer.

Turning, she thanked him politely for her lunch. Before she could dash out the door, he captured her hand. "May I take you out tonight?"

What gall! Stacy's mind rebelled. *He invites one girl out for lunch and then another for the evening!*

"Your father told me you were probably free when I talked to him earlier. He mentioned that you had stepped out of the office to deliver some memos for him. As a matter of fact, I was on my way over to your office when I met Jennifer, and she persuaded me to join her for lunch."

Some persuasion! She glanced back at the blonde, who was deftly applying a fresh layer of crimson lipstick to her pursed lips.

Undaunted by Stacy's silence, Drew continued smoothly: "I'll pick you up at six-thirty."

She recovered her voice. Peeved at his high-handedness, Stacy asked pertly, "Where are we going?"

"Out to dinner." He disparagingly surveyed her navy polyester pantsuit. "So wear a dress."

"Any more requests?"

"None that I can suggest right now," he drawled

suggestively, then smiled maddeningly at her rise in color.

"Until tonight." His lips brushed her cheek, scorching the skin with his touch, and she hurried through the entrance to escape from his vexing presence.

That evening, standing in front of her closet dressed in a lacy bra and bikini panties, Stacy's hand hovered over her selection of dresses, but then, defiantly, she grabbed a soft jersey jumpsuit and closed the door on her other choices. Quickly slipping into the outfit, she fastened the long row of gilt buttons up the front and at the cuffs of the full sleeves before she lost her courage.

Drew won't think this unfeminine, she noted mentally as she inspected the reflection in her full-length mirror. The narrow gold mesh belt emphasized her narrow waist, and the supple cinnamon fabric molded her full breasts and trim hips. Then she brushed her hair around her shoulders and fastened several gold chains which draped over the skin between the lapels.

She began to raise her hands to do up one more button, but she was distracted by the chiming of the doorbell. She picked up her skimpy little shoulder bag and slid the cord up over her arm and, thrusting any doubts aside, walked swiftly to the front hallway.

Slightly flushed, she flung open the heavy door and faced Drew, unable to speak over the thudding of her heart.

"Hello, Stacy." His eyes raked over her slowly from head to foot before he quirked an eyebrow. "Has your father seen you in that?"

Stunned by his uninhibited perusal and now his comment, Stacy struggled for an answer. Gathering her wits, she straightened her shoulders and lifted her chin. "No. Daddy is out for the evening—but he's never criticized my taste."

"He should when he sees you in that."

She tossed her head, causing the fabric to strain across her breasts. "It's very comfortable."

"I'm sure it is," he said impudently, eyeing the deep cleavage. "Ready?"

"Certainly."

When they were settled in the car, Stacy twisted to face him. "Where are we going?" Her stomach was starting to protest its empty state, and she hoped that they would not be driving far.

"I thought a home-cooked meal would be nice. . . . I've been eating out too much lately." His eyes flickered down at her. "So we're going to my place."

"Oh, really?" she said with as much aplomb as she could muster. She had not reckoned on this!

"Yes. I need to know if my future wife is as skilled in the kitchen as she assured me she was." She did not detect his mischievous gleam.

"That's hardly relevant under the circumstances."

"You never know. . . . If you can cook as well as you look, I might not be able to resist."

"I'm sure many girls could fill both those requirements."

"Not as well as you." As they were stopped at a traffic light, his smoky eyes intimately roamed down her curves.

Grateful for the dim light which concealed her burning cheeks, Stacy broke away from his smoldering gaze and, looking out the windshield, prosaically pointed out, "The light has changed."

"Thanks." He shifted gears, his sinewy forearm brushing her thigh. She edged slightly closer to the door to conceal her quivering response to his fleeting contact.

By his husky chuckle she realized that her maneuver had not gone unnoticed. "Take it easy . . . I never make love on an empty stomach . . . or in a car."

"That relieves me considerably," she returned dryly, unwilling to give him the satisfaction of upsetting her further. He was not the type of man to take advantage of her innocence, she assured herself firmly, recalling his preference for experienced women who would satisfy his male needs without the encumbrance of marriage.

A quarter of an hour later, he halted the car outside a row of contemporary town houses, each facade individualistically decorated.

Preceding Drew into the hallway, she immediately noticed the carpeted staircase leading to the second floor, and, she assumed, the master bedroom. Pulling her mind away from that particular direction, she saw through an arched doorway an L-shaped room. The masculine decor was explicit in the deep brown leather chairs and sofa. A glass and chrome room divider housed a stereo unit separating the living space from the dining area, and several modern prints hung on the walls, adding to the unreal feeling that she was stepping into a page of a decorator's manual.

"The kitchen's through that door." Drew pointed down the hall. "There's an apron hanging behind it. You don't want to spoil that . . . outfit."

"You are well prepared."

"Of course," he returned, unperturbed by her scathing tone.

Her polished nails dug into her palms, but before she could think of an appropriately biting retort, he laughed down at her, the sound springing from deep within his powerful chest. "Come. Keep me company while I put on the steaks." His eyes held a teasing glint. "All that needs doing is to broil the steaks and put dressing on the salad—I've even set the table."

"You were putting me on. . . ."

"And you rose so beautifully to the bait."

She flashed him a rueful grin but quickly lowered her lashes as she felt her nerves start to tingle under his potent gaze. Shrugging off his black sport coat, he dropped it on a nearby chair, exposing the rib-knit grey turtleneck hugging the rigid muscles of his chest and tucked into tartan slacks. "Come on, I'm getting hungry." Then, leaving her to follow, he strode back to the kitchen. He went straight to the refrigerator and brought out a package of steaks with one hand and in the other grasped a wooden bowl filled with crisp pieces of lettuce mixed with bright slices of carrots and tomatoes. He nudged the door closed with his elbow and spread the items out on the counter.

Looking over his shoulder to the girl standing just inside the room, he said, "Why don't you mix the dressing? All you need is up there." He inclined his head to the left toward a cabinet as he pulled out a drawer and produced a carving knive and a set of salad utensils. "I'll prepare the steaks."

Silently, Stacy followed his directions. Inside were neatly arranged bottles of spices, oil and vinegar, and to one side a cruet. "Do you have any preferences?"

"Just not too heavy on the oil."

"Okay." Her eyes kept drifting away from her task, observing his deft movements. As the minutes ticked away she felt drawn into the intimate atmosphere created when two people worked side by side on such prosaic chores. *It would be like this if we were married*, she mused. Then, troubled by the trend of her thoughts, she vigorously shook the cruet.

"I think it's mixed." She felt his warm breath caress her right ear lobe. He had put the steaks under the broiler and now stood beside her.

"I like the ingredients to be thoroughly mixed."

"You looked as though you were attacking it."

Ignoring his gibe, she poured the dressing on the salad. "I'm finished. Should I carry it through?"

"Go ahead. We'll start on it while the steaks broil. I've a couple of potatoes baking to go with them."

After she set the bowl down between the places arranged at one corner of the plate-glass table, she slipped into the cushioned chair Drew held for her. "I couldn't have done better myself," she said lightly.

"My mother taught me to be self-reliant." Drew filled two glasses with a red wine and handed one to Stacy.

"Mmm, this is good. Thank you. You never told me—where does your mother live?" Her eyes swung around the room. "Obviously, not here."

"No." The corner of his mouth lifted. "She has a house down the coast in Rockport. She spends most of her time painting."

"Does she ever visit you?"

"Now and then. She'll be in town in a week or two, so she can meet you."

"Me!" Her voice rose. "Why me?" She hastily lowered a forkful of salad and met his eyes— glimmering with amusement. "There's nothing funny about it!"

"What mother could resist meeting her son's fiancée?"

"You told her?" Stacy uttered in disbelief.

"Certainly . . ."

"But why make this more complicated than it already is?"

"She was bound to find out. I figured the news should come from me. . . . We've nothing to hide. . . . Excuse me; the steaks need turning."

By the time he reappeared, Stacy had regained control of her shaken nerves and apologized as he sat down. "I'm sorry I reacted so badly. It never occurred to me that your mother would have to be brought into this."

"Don't worry. Everything will work out in the end." His voice carried such conviction that, for some inexplicable reason, she was reassured.

The remainder of the meal passed smoothly; talk was minimal as they devoured the tender meat and russet potatoes smothered in butter. Replete, Stacy tentatively offered to wash the dishes.

"Don't bother. They can wait until the morning, when my cleaning woman comes in."

"How convenient. . . . Does she work every Saturday morning?"

"Usually."

Checking her train of thought, she rose to her feet and removed the plates, carrying them to the sink. She stalled for time by scraping them off and putting them in to soak. She heard Drew come up behind her and tilted her head up. "It's always easier if the food hasn't dried on them."

"I'm sure Mrs. Davies will be grateful. . . . Are you done?"

"Yes." She carefully wiped her damp hands on a paper towel and bent over, tossing it in with the rest of the trash, aware of his observing every movement.

"Let's go into the living room so we can listen to the stereo."

Hesitating in the doorway to consider her options, she glanced at Drew, who, she judged by his aggravating smile, expected her to choose the security of the single chair. Refusing to let him intimidate her, she sat down at one end of the sofa, unconsciously stretching out both arms, thus forming an effective barrier.

Surprised and a bit relieved, Stacy watched as Drew settled into the deep cushions of one of the chairs, comfortably stretching out his legs and crossing them at the ankles, his hands loosely clasped in his lap.

"Tell me what you've been up to this week." He continued teasingly, "Any old boyfriends been after you to reconsider?"

"What makes you say that?"

"Paul Elmwood." Drew's voice was now edged with steel.

"Who?" The color rose in Stacy's cheeks at her feeble attempt at evasion.

"You heard me. . . . Surely you haven't forgotten him?" His lids drooped over his eyes so they were narrow slits of darkness.

"No. I believe I told you earlier that he was a friend," she said with a touch of hauteur.

"And he hasn't said anything more about your engagement?" She saw the muscles of his jaw tighten as he leaned forward, intimidating her with his latent strength.

More bravely than she felt, she told him, "Whatever he said is my business, not yours."

His tone softened and he eased back in the chair. "That's right . . . just so he isn't pestering you."

"No. As a matter of fact, I haven't seen much of him."

"Good." She heard the ring of self-satisfaction in his voice. Then he dropped the subject and asked instead, "How do you like the music?"

Stacy had already perceived that the tunes were a selection of scores from various Broadway musicals and motion pictures; the haunting theme from *Romeo and Juliet* was gently teasing her senses. "It's very nice." With that, she closed her eyes, blocking out his chiseled profile and allowing the music to flow over her.

She was so absorbed in the music that she was not aware of any movement until a tingling sensation at the

nape of her neck warned her a second before she felt
the cushion compress under his added weight and her
nostrils caught his tangy, masculine scent. Her dark
lashes lifted and she saw Drew watching her, ensnaring
her in his spell; her pulse quickened as she waited
uncertainly for his next move, her feminine instincts
clamoring their alarm, but she was helpless to break the
compelling fascination of those penetrating eyes.

His strong, sinewy arms reached out and with one
lightning movement shifted her body so that she lay
helplessly across his lap, her soft breasts crushed
against his chest. Her throat felt dry, her breath ragged
as he murmured, "Darling, Stacy," an instant before
his lips took possession of her mouth. Waves of heat
spread throughout her body as he probed the secret
recesses of her mouth with the warm moistness of his
tongue. Tentatively, her hands explored the rippling
muscles of his back with its ribbed covering while he
drew her even closer, pressing one hand at the curve of
her spine as his other fingers fondled the sensitive skin
beneath her hair. Her heart pounded against her ribs
and she sucked in a deep, quivering breath as he
released her lips, descending along her chin and
downward to the pulse beating frantically at the base of
her throat, then on to the shadow between her breasts.

Moaning deep within her throat, Stacy felt his
caresses carry her far beyond her normal control, her
primitive instincts taking over. Her fingers discovered
his shirt had escaped from the confining waistband and
she slid her hands sensuously up across the firm skin of
his back, feeling the trembling awareness of his aroused
body. He freed several buttons and now his mouth
traced a line across the fullness of her right breast and,
pushing aside the flimsy lace bra, he covered the taut,
rosy tip.

Slowly, Stacy lifted her lids as cool air tingled on her

exposed skin. Drew's hand cupped her chin and his passion glazed eyes searched her face. He muttered thickly, "I want you, Stacy. . . ." With a sharp intake of breath, her mind cleared for just an instant before he kissed her pliant lips, resuming his erotic assault on her senses.

The harsh ringing of the telephone abruptly penetrated their consciousness. "Damn!" Drew swore violently as he lifted her off his lap and pushed her gently back onto the cushions.

Suddenly it was like awakening from a dream into harsh reality. She watched him rake his fingers through his disheveled hair and then casually shove his shirttail back into his pants as he strode over to answer the demanding summons.

"Yes," he said hoarsely and stood listening, his coiled strength prepared for action.

Embarrassed now by her shameless behavior, Stacy frantically readjusted her clothing, her shaking hands fumbling over the slippery fabric. She refused to allow her brain to dwell on what had almost happened. She was safe now, her virtue still intact; the phone call had exorcised her wanton temptation.

Dully, she heard Drew's voice from across the room. "Okay, I'll get right on it." He slammed down the receiver and turned to Stacy. "There's an emergency. I've got to fly down the coast tonight."

Mustering her wits, Stacy said with a false bravado, "I understand."

"Stacy, I don't want to leave." He ground out the words.

"You might say I was saved by the bell." Her attempted lightness fell flat.

"Don't joke!" His voice was harsh. "You're not that kind of girl!"

"Oh, really?" She added silently, *Well, then, what*

*kind am I? I come willingly to a man's apartment, and
when he starts to put the make on me I don't do anything
to stop him.*

He cut into her thoughts. "Look, I'll take you
home," he said, running an exasperated hand through
his thick hair.

Recoiling from his grudging solicitude, she suggested, "You could call a cab."

"No, I won't."

The leisurely pace of the early evening was gone; the
car rushed through the night until it screeched to a halt
before the apartment.

"Take care." She flung the words over her shoulder
as she jumped out and slammed the door. Running up
the steps, she heard the sports car roar off into the
night. At the top of the flight she paused, carefully
wiping away all traces of the tears which had trickled
down her cheeks.

Only the hallway light was on and she thankfully
flipped it off and made her way through the concealing
darkness to the sanctuary of her room. Carelessly
tossing her clothes over a chair, she climbed wearily
into bed and pulled up the covers. Huddled there in the
protective blackness, she squeezed her eyes shut, trying
to dam the humiliating swell of tears, and with them
came the shattering realization that she had fallen in
love with Drew. "Oh, God . . . what am I to do?" she
whispered, fervently aware that, though she cared for
him, all he felt was the need to slake his carnal desires.
She buried her face in the pillow, Drew's seductive
words echoing shamefully in her mind until the solace
of sleep blotted out her aching pain.

Chapter Seven

Stacy had just finished wrapping her hair in a terry towel when the doorbell chimed. Slipping into a velour wrap robe, she ran lightly to the front door and swung it open.

"Katie! It's so good to see you—come on in." She practically dragged the other girl into the hallway.

"Hi, Stacy. I hope you don't mind my dropping by like this."

"Not at all." Stacy closed the door with a muffled thud and turned back to Katie, who was hesitating in the hallway.

"You haven't any plans for this evening?"

Stacy fingered the damp towel. "I've just washed my hair—not a very thrilling task."

"Oh. I thought you might be getting ready for a date with Drew."

"No, he's still out of town." Her eyes clouded.

"How long is he going to be gone?"

She fixed a smile on her face and answered, "I'm not sure. Let's go sit down in the living room, if you don't mind my informal attire."

Katie chuckled. "Of course not." They went into the living room. Katie sat on the sofa, one hand absently fingering the binding while Stacy curled up in an armchair.

"Can I offer you anything to drink?" She half-rose in her seat, but settled back as Katie shook her head. "So what are you doing out this evening?"

Katie glanced up warily. "I just felt the need for some company and took a chance that you'd be home."

"Where's your mother?"

Katie's eyes widened in surprise. "Didn't you know? Mom is out with your father."

"Oh, ho, so that's where he went." Stacy grinned.

"He's taking her out to a show."

"The old fox. He was very close-mouthed about his plans. He gave me the impression he was attending a business function."

"You're not upset?"

Stacy smiled broadly, her eyes sparkling. "Are you kidding? It's perfect!"

Katie nodded. "Maybe he thought you wouldn't understand."

"Well, I'll have to set him straight," she said firmly. Then, with an amused glance at Katie, she added, "Don't worry. I'll be very subtle. I won't even mention that you"—she pointed an accusing finger—"spilled the beans." She chuckled at the other girl's expression of mock horror.

"Oh, thank you," Katie said dramatically, clasping her hands to her breast. "They must never know of our scheming."

Both girls fell into a fit of giggles. Slowly, Stacy

recovered, wiping tears of mirth from her long lashes. "Oh . . . if they only knew . . . that Sunday we had you to dinner—we were such good little girls to help in the kitchen."

"And left them . . . alone."

Sobering for a moment, Stacy added with a touch of satisfaction, "I'm glad it's working out."

"Yes. Mom's needed someone to make her take an interest in life again."

"That goes doubly for Dad." She paused thoughtfully. "He's been too wrapped up in his work." Rubbing her palms together, she added lightheartedly, "Now that they're taken care of, how about you?" A betraying flush spread over Katie's cheeks as she picked at a loose thread. "Are you keeping something from me?"

A moment passed before Katie stammered out, "I've been seeing quite a lot of Paul Elmwood." She looked up and said apologetically, "You don't mind, do you, Stacy?"

"Mind? Me? Not at all."

Katie appeared relieved, her expression lightened, but she still persisted: "But didn't you used to date him?"

"Yes," Stacy admitted honestly, "but it was never serious. Besides, I'm engaged to Drew." She spoke convincingly, but felt a guilty pang over her deception.

"Well, of course. It's just that I've wondered . . . Paul speaks of you often."

"So?"

"So"—Katie looked straight into her friend's eyes— "sometimes I think he's still interested in you and just takes me out because there's no one else."

"Oh, come on, Katie. You're a cute girl. Paul wouldn't be taking you out unless he wanted to."

Her lips curled up. "Thanks, Stacy."

"I mean it. You just need a shot of self-confidence."

"I suppose."

"If you don't believe me, take a good look in the mirror when you get home." She contemplated Katie's bouncy curls and big blue eyes and said speculatively, "I don't know if Paul is good enough for you."

"That's because you're prejudiced," Katie responded with a return of her usual good humor.

Stacy smiled. "Oh, am I?"

"Of course you are. Since you fell for Drew, you don't think any other man is—to use your phrase—'good enough.'"

"Is that it?" she murmured, her mind slowly absorbing Katie's reasoning. Then, with a rueful grin, she asked, "Well, then, you tell me, why is Paul so special? I've never noticed anything, and I've worked with him for over two years."

"I guess you were waiting till the right man came along."

If you only knew! Stacy mused. Then, uneasy with the trend of the conversation, she directed it away from herself by asking, "Tell me, where has Paul taken you out? Anyplace special?" Thus, she effectively kept Katie chatting about her own doings until she decided it was time to go back home.

Choosing not to wait up for her father, Stacy prepared for bed, carefully keeping her troubled thoughts at bay. But as had happened before, when she lay down, Drew's image immediately popped into mind, and with a pang of regret she acknowledged that her love for him was futile. He was not the type to settle down, and prolonging their association was not only useless, but dangerous. His sensual appeal strained her moral concepts and it shamed her to admit that she had smugly assumed that they would protect her from any man's advances. Now she realized that if she wanted to survive this "engagement" unscathed she would have to terminate it quickly or the next time Drew tempted her she might not be so lucky. Just before sleep overtook her, she resolved to confront Drew about calling it off.

If she cherished hopes that she could quickly carry out her decision, she was doomed to be disappointed. Mid-morning the next day she received a phone call which sealed the fate of her plan.

After she identified herself, the woman on the other end of the line said, "Oh, Stacy, I'm glad I reached you. I'm Mrs. Montgomery. Perhaps Drew has mentioned me?"

Stacy paused to think, but could not recall the name. "I'm sorry, Mrs. Montgomery, Drew hasn't."

"Oh, how like a man," she replied in exasperation. Then, with subtle charm, she said, "Please call me Estelle. My husband and I are good friends of the Pitmans. We'd like to give an engagement party for you and Drew a week from Friday."

Stacy forced some enthusiasm into her voice. "That's very kind of you, but I don't know what Drew's schedule is at the moment." It flashed through her mind that there might be a remote chance that the party could be postponed and, just possibly, never take place at all! But Estelle Montgomery's next words destroyed her wishful thinking.

"Drew's mother has been in touch with me and her son, and the date we selected is agreeable to them. I said I'd check with you, but I presumed Drew would warn you."

"No, he hasn't." And, giving in to the inevitable, she added reluctantly, "But that evening is fine with me."

"Good. My husband's away today. Perhaps you could come over to my home this evening and we could discuss the arrangements after dinner."

Stacy accepted the invitation, and after taking down

specific directions for finding the Montgomerys' house, she replaced the receiver and sat staring into space. Her thoughts revolved around the party. Eventually, she concluded that with Drew's mother already planning to attend, little could prevent it—better by far to get it over with as soon as possible. At least, if she confined their dates to public functions, she assured herself, she could take steps to avoid being alone with Drew. No more moonlit walks or dinners *à deux* at his place!

That evening, after work, Stacy hurried home through the gathering dusk. The sun's dying rays streaked the sky with tongues of flame. Prior to leaving the office, she had apprised her father of her invitation and had learned that he was going out too.

Upon being informed of his plans, Stacy had said, "Again?" Her eyes were twinkling.

He gazed at her suspiciously. "Yes. I'm having dinner with a friend."

"Anyone I know?" she probed, hoping that he would confide in her. It had troubled her that their close relationship had deteriorated since her engagement to Drew.

Her father shifted in his chair, then said with some asperity, "Yes. It's Muriel Goodwin."

"Why, Dad, that's marvelous!" She tried to appear surprised by his disclosure, but apparently it did not succeed because her father lifted one brow. "I get the feeling this news comes as no surprise."

Facing her father's discerning gaze, Stacy said, "I confess." She smiled mischievously. "I have my sources." She paused. "I'm a little disappointed that you didn't tell me sooner."

Self-consciously, he ran a finger along the inside of his collar. "There's nothing to tell; Muriel and I have known each other for years."

"Uh-huh. That's why you never mentioned the name of your 'companion.'"

"I wasn't trying to conceal it," he defended. "Didn't know you'd find it so important."

She smiled affectionately. "Well, anyway, I'm glad you're not working such long hours. Since you'll be out I won't plan any dinner."

"That's fine. I'll pick up something after I finish here." He turned his attention to the papers on his desk.

"Okay. Bye, Dad." She turned and walked back into her office, and after straightening up her desk, she went home to get her car.

She was not really looking forward to this meeting, but, as it turned out, things went smoothly. Mrs. Montgomery could not have been more kind or considerate. During a light meal and a tour of the gorgeously decorated home, Estelle explained her ideas for the party and encouraged Stacy to contribute her suggestions. The only sour note of the evening occurred after they had returned to the sumptuous living room and Estelle handed her the guest list.

"I'm sure there are several names you'd like to add, but these are the ones I've compiled so far. I've taken the liberty of addressing the invitations, and I have more ready for your additions."

Stacy scanned the list, pleased with the choices, until she read Jennifer Hyatt's name. Suddenly feeling almost as though someone had knocked the wind out of her, she clutched the sheet and took a deep breath. She hadn't been prepared for this! *How dare Drew invite his girl friend to our engagement party!* Stacy seethed. Jennifer had marred the other party, and Stacy knew instinctively that she would try to jinx this one. But her hands were tied. She was helpless. The invitation was all ready, and she couldn't think of any adequate excuse to rescind it. *Well, at least I'll be prepared,* she thought stoutly. *Forewarned is forearmed.*

The days prior to the party slipped by, one pretty much like another. Her decision made to finish the engagement, Stacy stubbornly suppressed thoughts of Drew by working hard all day, and every evening she took advantage of the milder weather and jogged. By the time she was ready for bed, her body was exhausted sufficiently enough for her to sleep.

The only break in the pattern occurred four days before the party. She had returned from jogging and was preparing for a bath when the telephone rang. She picked it up on the second ring.

"Hello." Her heart skipped a beat as Drew's voice came over the wire.

"Hi, Stacy. Remember me?" Her legs gave way and she plunked down on the bed. Then, gathering her wits, she asked, "Who is this? Tom, Dick . . . or Harry?" She strove to make her tone flippant when all the while her senses were clamoring.

"Guess again. . . ."

"Could it possibly be Drew Pitman?"

"Right." He chuckled. "You were expecting someone else?"

"Well, my social calendar has been so busy lately . . ." She let her sentence trail off ambiguously.

"Oh, really?" He laughed. "And here I thought you were pining away until I came home."

"And when is that?" Stacy couldn't help asking.

"The day before the Montgomerys' party. I can't miss that."

"No, you can't, since you chose the date." A touch of annoyance crept into her voice.

"Do I detect a note of censure?"

Ire bubbled up. "Why should you? Just because I wasn't consulted . . ." She stopped; she wouldn't bicker over the phone.

"It was the best we could do under the circumstances," he explained. "Have you met our hostess?"

"Yes. Estelle's been very thoughtful. She invited me over to her home and we discussed all of the arrangements."

"Good. Estelle Montgomery is very adept at handling these functions. Any other news?"

Shifting uneasily on the edge of the bed, Stacy thought of her decision, but told him, "Nothing that can't wait."

"Okay. Plan on my picking you up at seven. That way we'll have a chance to visit with Mother."

"That will be fine. See you then. . . . Bye, Drew."

"So long." The line went dead and Stacy carefully replaced the receiver and then propped her chin on her hand, her forehead pleating in a frown. Everything had become so complicated. In just a few days she had to meet Drew's mother and more family friends, each one expecting her to be a radiantly happy bride-to-be. If she had known of the ramifications back when Drew first made his announcement, she would have insisted on telling the truth; far better to have faced her father's wrath. She stood up, walked into the bathroom, slid out of her robe, and sank down into the steaming tub.

Well, she mused, *hindsight isn't going to help. Things have gone too far to back out now. But soon,* she assured herself, *everything will be back to normal.* She tried not to contemplate what "normal" would mean; never to see Drew, nor be held in his arms. She eased her limbs into a comfortable position and let the heat soak into her aching muscles, closing her eyes, but it wasn't so easy to close her mind to her arousing memories.

The night of the party Stacy took considerable care with her appearance. She had selected one of her favorite dresses to bolster her confidence; it was made from a supple ivory fabric which draped gracefully in a cowl neckline across the front and dipped down in the back to expose her smooth, creamy skin. The bodice clung from her shoulders to her waist and then hung in soft folds so that as she moved, it swished around her ankles. To complete the effect she arranged her hair in a topknot and had to apply her makeup more than once before she was satisfied.

She was surveying the final results in her full-length mirror when she heard the sound of the doorbell. With a feeling of trepidation, she collected her lacy shawl and evening bag and left the security of her room.

As she walked toward the living room, she saw Drew with his back to her, talking to her father as they waited. For a moment she observed him unnoticed. He wore a black evening suit with an unmistakable air of panache. The dark material outlined his broad shoulders and lean hips, and contrasted sharply with his blond hair. Stacy could not deny that he was the best-looking man she had ever dated.

She reined in her thoughts as, upon detecting her presence, he turned to face her.

"Good evening, Drew," she greeted him coolly, daring to meet his enigmatic smile with one of her own.

"Hello, Stacy. You look . . . lovely." As he spoke, he covered the space between them and grasped her bare upper arms, pulling her against his ruffled shirt. Her nostrils filled with his masculine scent as he lowered his head to kiss her.

Stacy tried to keep her mouth rigid, but as his warm

lips gently teased her mouth she discovered to her consternation that she could not restrain her response.

When he released her, he smiled knowingly before he turned his attention to Bob. *Darn him!* she thought furiously. *Why does he have this effect on me?* She strove to regain her former coolness, but it was impossible since he had captured one hand and gently massaged the inside of her wrist with his thumb. It sent a tingling awareness up her arm and throughout her body. Oblivious to the men's exchange of words, Stacy glanced up and saw a glimmer of unholy amusement in Drew's eyes and she knew he sensed her involuntary reaction to his sensual caress.

Drew's voice caught her attention as he said, "We'll see you later, Bob." Then he looked down at her, his eyes still alight. "Ready?"

"Yes." She slid her shawl over her shoulders and said to her father, "You're driving yourself?"

Bob laughed and Stacy stared at him, confused. "You gave yourself away, kitten. You were so wrapped up in seeing Drew again you didn't listen. I've explained that I would be escorting Muriel to the party."

"Katie's coming, isn't she?"

"Yes, of course. Her date will bring her."

"Oh, good . . ."

"I think we'd better start moving or everyone will arrive before us, and remember, Mother wants to meet you privately."

"I'm looking forward to it." Her voice came out strained.

"Bye, Bob." Drew steered Stacy toward the door and whispered in her ear, "Little liar."

She scowled. "What do you mean?" she snapped when the door closed behind them.

"I got the distinct impression you don't relish going to this party. Or is it meeting Mother?"

"Both," she was forced to answer honestly.

"Well"—his eyes assessed her gown—"you needn't be concerned over your appearance."

"Thanks." The word came out with an edge of indifference.

"I meant that as a compliment." Now he was frowning, baffled by her tone.

"Good. . . . Shall we go?" She was pleased to have the upper hand for once. But this feeling was quickly lost as he spun her around to face him, sliding his hands under her shawl and up across her bare back.

"Did you miss me?"

"No."

"Liar," he breathed softly as he hugged her and covered her mouth with his own.

Shaken by his ardency, Stacy was reluctantly grateful for the support of his arm across her shoulders as they made their way down the open-tread steps.

After a brief drive they reached their destination. The Montgomerys' home was built along modern lines: long and low. All of the inner rooms had sliding-glass doors which opened onto a terrace where Estelle planned to have dancing.

The evening was perfect—cool but not chilly, a blanket of stars across the sky. Stacy felt a gentle breeze stir her hair as they approached the massive front door. Drew held his arm securely around her waist and she wondered irreverently if it was to ensure that she didn't bolt before confronting his mother. She smiled at the thought.

Drew glimpsed her whimsical smile. "Want to let me in on the joke?"

"Oh, it's nothing."

He dismissed it with a shrug of his shoulders and pressed firmly on the doorbell.

Mrs. Montgomery, elegantly attired in a midnight-blue evening dress, opened the door herself and welcomed them into the spacious terrazzo hallway. "Drew, dear boy, I'm pleased you and Stacy arrived early."

A distinguished-looking man just a few inches taller than Estelle came up and shook Drew's hand. "Good to see you, Drew." He turned his attention to Stacy. "And this, I assume, is Stacy."

His wife made the necessary introduction and he took Stacy's hand. "It's a pleasure to meet you, young lady. You've impressed my wife."

"Why . . . thank you, sir." She felt her cheeks begin to warm as she looked straight into John Montgomery's discerning eyes.

Estelle linked her arm through her husband's. "John, don't embarrass the poor girl." Then she informed them, "Dorothy will be along in a few minutes." She caught the sound of light footsteps and turned her head. "Ah . . . here she is now."

Stacy watched Drew's mother as she glided toward them, and she quickly revised her mental image. Somehow, she had assumed that she would be the stereotype of an artist instead of this cool, meticulously dressed lady. She wore a long, black gown whose deceptively simple style decried its superior design. Everything about her was immaculate, from her short, wavy hair to her pale-polished nails. The resemblance to her son was evident in her blonde hair touched with grey, her blue eyes, and the strong cheekbones.

"Sorry to keep you waiting," Drew's mother told the quartet. As she came abreast of her son, she patted his back, saying, "Hello, dear."

"Mother." He gave her a feather-light kiss and then said, "This is Stacy."

The older lady regarded her appraisingly as she

extended one slim hand. "My dear, I'm so pleased to meet you." With a swift glance to her son, she added, "You're just as pretty as Drew described you."

"Thank you, Mrs. Pitman." Her skin became warmer.

"Dorothy, please, we're almost family."

"Thank you . . . Dorothy." Instinctively, she felt an easing of her tension at his mother's cordiality.

"Dorothy, why don't you take these two to the study? There you can have some privacy until our guests arrive," Estelle suggested.

"That's a delightful idea. I need to get acquainted with this young woman." She smiled and took them both by the arm.

When they reached the study, Stacy gazed around appreciatively. A broad desk dominated the room, and around the walls were bookcases, and there was still room for a conversation grouping of tweed-upholstered furniture.

After they were seated, Stacy and Dorothy on the sofa, while Drew relaxed in an armchair, Dorothy explained, "I'm sorry I haven't been to Houston sooner, but I was involved with getting work done for an exhibit."

"That's all right. I understand."

"Actually, I was quite surprised when Drew told me." She smiled at her son. "I had about given up hope that he would ever marry."

"I'm not in my dotage yet, Mother."

"I should hope not!" she chuckled. "Then where would I be?"

"I expect you'll still be painting in your nineties."

"I do have a few years to go, then?"

"I don't need to tell you that you've never looked better."

"It's nice to hear, anyway." She leaned forward and

touched the hand resting on the low arm of the chair. "Have you told Stacy about my plans for tomorrow?"

"Not yet. I thought I'd leave it to you." Stacy was curious, her eyes wide as they flickered between mother and son.

Dorothy told her. "I have the day free tomorrow and I suggested to Drew that we go shopping at the Galeria."

"That sounds fine to me," she agreed, concealing a twinge of apprehension at spending several hours in this observant woman's company.

They continued to chat for several more minutes until Drew suggested that they rejoin their friends.

When Bob and Muriel arrived, Drew adroitly introduced everyone, and the well-mannered politeness of strangers was soon displaced by a mutual amicability.

As at the last party, Drew's and Stacy's attention was claimed by their friends, so it wasn't until well into the evening that Drew invited her to dance. Estelle had arranged for a mixture of fast and slow music so it would appeal to the various interests of her guests. Out under the canopy of stars, Stacy breathed deeply the azalea-scented air and gave herself up to the floating sensation created as she danced in Drew's warm embrace. She felt as though she could continue this way all night.

The music ceased and she came out of her dream with a thud when she heard Jennifer Hyatt practically purr near her ear, "Stacy, you don't mind if I steal your fiancé . . . for one dance." She wore a daringly cut snow-white dress which invited a man to admire her feminine charms. In comparison, Stacy felt almost dowdy.

"He's all yours," Stacy said, forcing her voice to sound nonchalant, and she accompanied her words with a carefree flick of her wrist. The music started almost at once and Stacy strolled to the side of the lamp-lit terrace, a strained smile fixed on her lips. Idly, her eyes searched the crowd for the dapper young man she had noticed earlier escorting Jennifer. She spotted him over at the bar, already appearing a bit worse for the liquor he had consumed. Deciding against approaching him, she hesitated, unsure what to do next. She didn't enjoy standing on the edge of the dancers like a forgotten wallflower.

Suddenly Paul was beside her and invited her to dance. She slipped into his arms but resisted his pressure to draw her in closer. "What's the matter, Stacy?" He caught her eyes. "Drew's interest cooling off?" He shifted his eyes deliberately to the couple drifting sensuously together a bit apart from the other dancers.

"I don't like your questions."

"Sorry, but I heard that tonight is the first time you've been out with him for two weeks."

"He's been working," she defended.

"Oh, really?" The innuendo in his voice was not lost on Stacy.

"If you're going to keep this up, I don't want to dance any longer." She moved out of his grasp, but before she could get away, Paul seized her arm and propelled her down the terrace steps to the velvet lawn.

"Paul, I want to go back." She tried to shrug off his hand.

"Not until we've talked."

"I have nothing to say to you."

They were now concealed from the others by the thick shrubs. "Stacy . . . Stacy. Open your eyes. Drew isn't in love with you."

"That's not for you to judge."

"But I can't allow you to get hurt . . . I care too

much." He tried to pull her into his arms, but she out-maneuvered him.

"No, Paul! Leave me alone! Someone might see us."

Unaware that another figure had silently tracked them, Stacy jumped guiltily when Drew's harsh voice ordered, "Shove off, Paul. I don't want you near my fiancée!" Stacy gazed anxiously at the face tightened in anger and the hands clenched at his sides as though itching to use them.

"Butt out. You're not wanted here," Paul sneered with blustering bravado.

"Oh, yeah?" Drew took a step forward, but Stacy blocked his way.

"Paul, please go!"

He glanced down into her pleading eyes and back to the menacing stare. "Okay . . . but if you need me . . ."

"She won't be needing you," Drew asserted as Paul, losing his daring, hastily retreated.

"Who invited him?" demanded Drew.

"I did," Stacy said staunchly.

"I don't want to see him touching you again."

"Oh, does it prick your male ego?"

He pierced her with a fiery glare, reached out, and captured her hands with his, pinning them behind her as he dragged her resisting body against the hard wall of his chest and fused his lips on hers, mercilessly asserting his domination. She felt her teeth grind into the inside of her mouth as she struggled ineffectually to break his binding hold. At last he shoved her away, his breath coming in ragged gasps.

Contemptuously, she wiped her swollen mouth with the back of her hand, tasting her own salty blood.

"Next time you won't get off so easily." His eyes burned into her.

"Excuse me." Stacy's voice dripped with acid, but

her body trembled. She pivoted on her heel and escaped back to the house.

By sheer instinct she found the bedroom reserved for female guests. Thankful that it was vacant when she entered, she sank down onto the nearest chair, breathing deeply until she had herself under control. Her wrap was on the bed and under it she found her evening bag. She took it over to the dressing table and, with a hand that shook only slightly, she applied a fresh coat of lipstick to her ravished mouth. Then, adding a light covering of powder, she whispered to the reflection, "There you go, my girl. Good as new." She smiled wryly and snapped the bag closed. She returned it to the satin-quilted bedspread, and as she started for the door, Jennifer sauntered in.

Just what I need! Stacy thought to herself. Aloud, she inquired politely, "Jennifer . . . are you enjoying the party?"

"Of course," she said archly.

"Good." Stacy moved closer to the door.

"Just a minute." A talon-like hand, with blood-red nails, shot out to capture her arm. "I want a minute of your time."

Stacy fixed her eyes on the restraining fingers and answered in frigid tones, "Let go of my arm."

The other girl instantly withdrew her hand as though she had singed her fingers, but then, regaining her poise, she said, "I trust you don't mind that Drew invited me tonight."

"No, of course not. We invited all of our friends." There was the merest hesitation before the word "friends."

"I'm glad you don't find it too awkward," she drawled insolently. "Drew and I are so 'close.' " She let her implication sink in and then added, "I suggested to him last week that it might be better if I stayed home, but he persuaded me to come."

Stacy could only stare blankly at the sleek blonde, something like pain tearing at her insides. Shaking her head to clear her vision, she saw the smug satisfaction in Jennifer's expression. And then, refusing to allow Jennifer to demoralize her, Stacy squared her shoulders. "Thank you for your concern. Now, excuse me. Drew is waiting."

"I wouldn't be too sure of that."

Ignoring the catty remark, Stacy opened the door, stepped through, and quietly closed it upon the vindictive woman's face.

The rest of the evening took on an unreal quality. Stacy assiduously avoided Drew until the last guest had departed and he escorted her home.

They covered the short drive in frigid silence, Stacy holding herself aloof while her mind grappled for a way to approach Drew to terminate the engagement. Her earlier decision was now confused by so many side issues. Since Drew had obviously misconstrued her behavior with Paul, he would assume her decision was based on Paul's imprecations. And Paul, once he found out the engagement was off, would erroneously conclude it was the result of his actions. And then there was Jennifer. Stacy admitted to herself that it was foolish, but her pride balked at allowing that female to think she had scored off her.

Her mind was so preoccupied that she was barely conscious of her movements until they were inside the apartment and Drew, his hands thrust into his pockets, said impatiently, "Are you going to explain what you and Paul were up to out in the bushes?"

She flinched under his sordid description, but intrepidly hissed, "Keep your voice down unless you want to wake up my father."

"Don't change the subject." His voice was a furious whisper, a muscle twitched in his cheek.

"What needs to be explained . . . ? I thought you knew it all," she challenged him.

"So you have no excuse for carrying on with Paul?" His eyes bored into her.

"And what about your behavior with Jennifer?"

For a moment he looked nonplussed, and then the rigid line of his mouth curled. "You're jealous . . . and you're trying to use Paul to get back at me."

"I am not! I was not."

He laughed deeply, the tension easing in his face.

"Ohhh . . ." She threw up her hands, her eyes blazing. "Think what you like . . . I'm going to bed. Close the door on your way out." She hurried to her room, but like a shot he came after her and, just as she flipped on the light switch, Drew grabbed her wrist and pulled her into the bedroom, shoving the door closed with his foot while spinning her around to face him.

"No one turns their back on me."

Stacy steadied herself, grinding her teeth together. His eyes narrowed on her quizzically. "Something tells me there's more to this than you're letting on. I'm waiting to be filled in."

"I don't care! Just . . . just leave me alone!" Her eyes flickered up at him and then down to the rug; she refused to reveal Jennifer's intimations.

"If I recall correctly, you appeared several minutes after Jennifer went off to powder her nose." He eyed her speculatively. "Did you girls have a pleasant chat?"

"I . . . I didn't see her."

"You're not a convincing liar." He ran a finger over her rounded jaw. "What could Jennifer say to upset you? Hmm . . ." He paused thoughtfully. "Did she mention seeing me in Dallas last week?" The guilty flutter of her lashes betrayed her, and he continued: "Did she also tell you the meeting was accidental? She was there on a photographic assignment and I spoke with her briefly before a man arrived for our business luncheon."

Her mind absorbed his words. His glib explanation fit all the pieces together neatly . . . perhaps too neatly? *Oh, damn! He's got me so mixed up!*

Drew cut into her thoughts. "Knowing Jennifer, I can assume there was more." He stared at her shrewdly as she glanced up in astonishment. "My guess is that she's implied there's more to our friendship."

Drew watched the telltale color flood into her cheeks. "So, I'm right."

Stacy winced at the scorn in his voice, but she could not tear her eyes away from his. "Just for the record, Jennifer is not my mistress."

There was a significant pause while Stacy's mind assimilated his statement, her eyes searching his face for any sign of duplicity. Finally, she took a ragged breath. "I'm sorry, Drew."

"So am I." He strode over to the door. "Pleasant dreams. . . ."

As the door flew shut, tears trickled unchecked down Stacy's cheeks. Drew's last words had held such a wealth of bitterness that she knew something vital to their relationship had foundered—trust. . . .

Chapter Eight

Standing on the sidewalk in front of the apartment, wearing a yellow shirtwaist dress, Stacy waited apprehensively for the Pitmans. She was oblivious to the beams of sunshine burning off the early morning haze and the scent of early spring flowers. She fiddled with the strap of her shoulder bag, scanning the street for a sign of Drew's car. After their blow-up last night, she was not anticipating the shopping trip with any pleasure since they would both be constrained to put on a good front for his mother.

Uneasy, her stomach churning, unsettled by the hastily consumed coffee and toast, Stacy recalled her last-minute conservation with her father.

She had risen late to avoid him, but just as she reached the hallway, ready to leave, Bob had intercepted her.

"I see you're set to go."

"That's right. I . . . I thought I'd wait outside for the

Pitmans so they won't have to bother finding a parking space. It's so crowded around here on Saturday morning with everyone sleeping in late."

If her father noticed the ill-concealed shadows under her eyes or her nervous fingers on the hair clip holding back her parted hair, he did not refer to it, but said instead, "You know, kitten, that if you ever need to talk, I'm here."

Stacy felt her eyes mist over. Without prying, he had let her know that he was willing to help and give her any support she needed. She placed her hands on his shoulders, stood on tiptoes, and kissed his cheek. Then, looking at his kind, familiar face, she said, "Thanks, Daddy . . . I appreciate that."

"I just want you to be happy. . . . I know it's hard for young people these days, but . . ." He studied her carefully, then said with a smile, "Don't get caught up by petty issues. These things have a way of resolving themselves if we give them time."

"That's good advice. Any more words of wisdom?" She tried to keep her words light.

But he sensed her inner turmoil, so he continued: "Just don't be too hasty to condemn. When you love someone it's easy for them to hurt you, and humans have a tendency to lash out in defense."

What can I say? she thought sadly. *He obviously overheard part of our argument.* "Thanks, Daddy. I'll keep it in mind."

"Good, and since you are so receptive, I'll add . . ." He smiled at her feigned grimace. "Don't let misunderstanding fester. If you don't talk it out, problems can build up out of proportion." He looked wisely down at his daughter. "You have a streak of impetuosity that doesn't always allow you enough time to think before you act."

"Ain't that the truth." She started to grin. "You know me very well."

His eyes crinkled at the corners. "I should. I've known you long enough. I can remember several episodes when you were a little girl. . . ."

"Oh, please don't bring them up," she pleaded.

"Okay." He kissed her cheek. "Enough said. . . . I'm planning on going over to Muriel's this afternoon. She's taken me up on my offer to help with her garden."

Feeling reprieved, Stacy said, "I'm glad you're going to get some fresh air. My advice to you is," she said cheekily, "don't overdo."

He responded drily, "Thanks. Now, why don't you get going before you give me any more pearls of wisdom?"

"Okay. Bye. . . . Take care."

And now, as she recognized Drew's black Corvette cruising up the street, the powerful throb of the engine announcing its arrival, she wondered whether she would have the chance to act on her father's advice.

As she climbed into the low, shiny car, Drew told her, "Mom's waiting at the entrance to Lord & Taylor." He shifted the car into gear and took off.

"Good thinking," she found herself responding with levity. "I didn't anticipate riding back there." She jerked a thumb in the direction of the small space between the seats and the rear window.

"You're just a bit too big for that maneuver." Drew had smiled, but now his jaw hardened and he threw her a piercing glance. "I think we have to talk." He pulled the car over to the side of the street, turned off the motor, and twisted toward Stacy, his open-necked sport shirt gaping open as he hooked his left arm across the steering wheel. The fresh scent of his after-shave teased her senses. "By the looks of you, I think you'll agree."

"Huh . . . ? What do you mean?"

One long blunt finger traced a line under her eyes. "You didn't sleep very well."

She tried to prevaricate. "We got home late . . ."

"And then had a row . . . Not particularly conducive to a good night's rest."

Stacy dropped her lashes, concealing the misery that haunted her.

"Look, we'll be spending the day together, so let's call a truce. We can't spoil Mother's last day here."

"When is she leaving?"

"In the morning. She's arranged to have dinner with friends who will pick her up later this afternoon. Have we got a deal?"

"It's okay by me."

"Thanks."

"You're welcome." He grinned at her absurd politeness and then restarted the engine.

Stacy sat quietly, assessing their agreement. Although she knew that they hadn't actually settled anything, she was unwilling to air their problems and upset the tenuous balance. Against her better judgment she could not resist enjoying this time with Drew, and she temporarily banished her worries about the future.

Minutes later, as they made their way through the Galeria, Stacy could hear the tapping of her heels and Drew's heavier tread on the tiled floor. It was still early; the stores had been open less than one hour, and as yet there were relatively few people crowding the corridors.

Just before they reached the store, Drew took her hand. "Smile."

Stacy glanced up and, reassured by his twinkling eyes, she lifted the corners of her mouth.

"That's better."

"Tell me, does your mother have anything particular she wants to buy?"

"I have no idea. Women just like to shop; they don't need another purpose."

"Spoken like a typical male."

He grinned. "I was coerced into this."

Her mouth twitched. "I'm glad you're taking it so well."

"Goodness has its own rewards."

"Oh, really . . . ? And what are they?"

"I won't enumerate them now." He smiled again and Stacy sensed it was safer to let his innuendo pass unchallenged.

They found Dorothy waiting just inside the entrance, wearing an informal dress of burgundy with navy trim.

She smiled up at her tall son. "I've just been looking around a bit. You were gone quite a while."

"Sorry if we kept you waiting."

"I had begun to think you might be lost."

"In two and a half blocks?" Drew quirked his eyebrow.

"You never know. . . . I was young once." Her eyes twinkled.

"In broad daylight? Mother, I'm surprised at you!"

"Oh, Drew!" She laughed. "Daylight has nothing to do with it."

Stacy joined in the laughter as Drew's blue eyes widened in mock amazement.

"You're corrupting this innocent young woman."

Dorothy raised her brow in the same imperious gesture as her son, and then, to Stacy, she said, "I'm sorry if I've embarrassed you. . . . Why don't we head on? It's so nice of Drew to accompany us; I don't want to give him any excuses to abandon us."

About an hour later they stopped for lunch and then

resumed their shopping. Drew was now carrying
several packages for his mother. Among other things,
she had bought some special painting supplies.

Stacy had been doing a lot of browsing, but hadn't
made a purchase when they arrived at one of the
smaller women's dress shops which displayed a large
selection of the new spring line of swimwear.

Dorothy found herself a delightful suit in deep
shades of pink and mauve, and she persuaded Stacy to
try on a Hawaiian-print bikini. Holding the wisps of
fabric in one hand, she picked up the matching wrap
and hurried into the dressing room, deliberately ignoring Drew's provocative glance.

She was unprepared for the reflection which met her
gaze in the full-length mirror. The fabric barely covered
the strategic parts, exposing a tantalizing amount of
skin at her rounded breasts and curving buttocks. *No
one would take you for a boy,* she told her other self,
astounded by the sexy image. She slipped on the short,
matching jacket, tying all three bows down the front.

"Stacy, we're waiting for you to model for us." She
heard Drew's voice come from just beyond the curtains. Admiring herself in the mirror was one thing;
facing Drew was another. She swallowed, gathering her
nerve, pushed aside the drapes, and stepped out. She
saw Drew leaning nonchalantly against a rack of
clothes, his hands thrust into his pockets, straining the
fabric across his muscular thighs.

Dorothy spoke first. "That's a darling jacket, perfect
for a pool or the beach."

"How 'bout the suit?" Drew drawled his words.

"It's fine . . . it fits."

"Aren't you going to show us?"

Tapping his shoulder reprovingly, Dorothy said,
"Stop it, Drew."

"Mother, I thought Stacy might value our opinion,"

he finished audaciously as he stepped in front of Stacy. In a blink of an eye he had untied the bows and was pushing the fabric back over her shoulders.

"I'll do it myself," she hissed. "Move back."

"Anything to oblige." His lazy smile was unrepentant, and he never let his eyes stray as she shrugged off the jacket.

Stacy could feel the heat from the blood rushing to the surface of her skin while Drew's eyes wandered down her body.

"All you need is a tan."

Dorothy was enthusiastic. "It looks marvelous. Oh, I envy you young girls. You can get away with wearing a suit like that."

"Should we buy you one, Mother?" He winked at Stacy. "I'm sure your figure is a lot better than many we see on the beaches."

"Oh, no . . . my days for a bikini are over."

"I'll go change," Stacy told them, holding the jacket in front of her like a shield.

"It's a shame to cover it up. We'll plan a trip to the beach as soon as the weather warms up." Drew's eyes captured hers and she was unsure how to take his offer. He sounded sincere . . . but perhaps it was affected just for his mother. She wrenched her eyes away, mumbled her agreement, and then scurried back behind the curtains.

Once she had dressed, she carried the articles over to the cash desk and wrote a check for her purchases, refusing to consider when she might have the opportunity to wear them.

The three of them had covered several more shops when Dorothy checked her watch. "I think we should start walking to the Houston Oaks Hotel. If we take these stairs, we'll come out near the lobby. I arranged to meet the Campbells there at four."

They reached the hotel lobby in a few minutes and her son asked, "Will I see you again before you leave?"

"No. I plan to drive home first thing in the morning."

"Do you have enough gas? Many stations are closed on Sunday."

"Yes, dear, I filled the car yesterday. After dinner the Montgomerys are stopping by and they'll take me back to their home. Satisfied?"

He gave a lopsided grin. "Yes, as usual you have everything well organized."

"Where do you think you got your organizational ability?"

"From Dad," he quipped.

"Oh, ho . . . thanks." She turned to Stacy. "Do you think you can handle this patronizing son of mine?"

"I'll try."

"Well, I wish you good luck." She gave her son a baleful glance. "I like this young lady, so don't scare her off before the wedding. . . . I think I'm even looking forward to being a grandmother."

"Slow down! First I have to get the ring on her finger."

"Well, don't take too long."

"I won't."

Drew's words acted like a swift blow to Stacy's heart. She understood it was all part of the act, but simultaneously she wished he had spoken the truth.

While they were talking, Dorothy's friends pulled up outside the glass doors, and Drew's mother, observing their arrival, said to Stacy, "I'm glad we had this chance to get to know each other a little better." She hugged the girl. "Let me know when the wedding is to be."

"Yes, of course. Have a good trip back."

"Thank you, dear." And to Drew: "Take care of yourself, son." She kissed him lightly on the cheek. "You've found yourself a wonderful girl."

Drew put his arm around Stacy's shoulders, drawing her close. "Yes, I know." He glanced down at Stacy and then back to his mother. "Thanks for making the drive up, and thank the Montgomerys again for all their trouble."

"They were happy to do it. Well, good-bye for now."

Drew's and Stacy's voices blended as they bade her farewell. He kept his arm where it was even after Dorothy had waved and the car moved away.

He gave her a considering look. "That wasn't so bad, was it?"

"No, of course not. I like your mother."

"Good. . . . Well, where would you like to go now? And don't say home. This weather is too good to waste."

Inordinately pleased, Stacy suggested, "We could go for a drive in the country."

"What! Haven't you heard of the gasoline shortage?" His eyes crinkled as he grinned. "I have an idea. . . ."

"What is it?"

"I'll let it be a surprise."

A little frustrated, she said, "You like surprises, don't you?"

"Yup. Anticipation is half the enjoyment. Come on, let's go find my car."

Stacy was kept in suspense as Drew drove around the highway loop and exited downtown. It wasn't until they drove north past the medical center that she began to have a glimmer of an idea.

As the tires crunched through the loose gravel in the parking lot, Stacy said enthusiastically, "I haven't been to Herman Park in ages."

"Well, it isn't the country, but there are plenty of trees."

The grass was springy beneath their feet, and Drew

imprisoned one of Stacy's hands in his own brown one as they strolled under the great old oak trees.

Everywhere she looked she saw children—playing, laughing, fighting. There were even a few people on horseback from the nearby livery stable.

"Just a minute." Drew dropped Stacy's hand and loped away. She followed him with her eyes. His slacks outlined his muscular legs with each stride and the knit shirt stretched over the whipcord muscles of his back. As he slowed to a stop before the hot dog stand, he brushed his blond hair back from his forehead.

Within five minutes he returned, carrying three hot dogs in one large hand and a can of soft drink in the other.

"Hungry?"

"What if I said no . . . ?"

"Then I'd eat them myself."

"Oh, no, I can't let you do that." Playfully, she grabbed one and skipped back, biting into the end with her strong, white teeth. She made a face as the mustard oozed out and ran the tip of her tongue around her lips.

"You missed a spot." Drew leaned forward and with his tongue flicked the spot beside her mouth. "Hmm. Interesting flavor." Drew licked his own lips and smiled impudently as Stacy, her pulses racing from the fleeting contact, recovered her equilibrium.

"Didn't you bring any napkins?"

"Don't need any, do we?" He gave her an amused glance.

"Guess not." She diverted her eyes and watched the playing children. She munched on the rest of her hot dog and then, in the absence of napkins, licked her fingers. Drew had opened the can of cola and offered it to her.

"Thanks." The effervescent bubbles cooled her mouth and throat and she handed it back to him, absently listening to some pre-schoolers at the nearby swings. She smiled to herself as she heard a little girl who looked to be about five instructing her younger brother.

"Hold on, Stuart, so I can push you."

"No," came a surprisingly deep voice.

"I won't be your sister anymore," she tried threatening.

"No!"

Shaking her head in amusement, Stacy walked over and offered, "Can I help?"

The big brown eyes gazed soulfully up at her. "He won't hold on so I can push him."

"Maybe he doesn't want to swing," she suggested seriously, crouching down to the child's level.

"Yes, he does; he won't obey me."

"Can I try?"

This was met with a vigorous nod. Stacy turned to the little boy and said, "Stuart, do you want me to push you?" He just gave her a blank look, so she tried again: "Do you want to swing?"

Slowly, he nodded his head. Hallelujah! She had found the right phrase. Putting one small hand around each of the swing's chains, she warned him, "Hold on tight!"

She pushed, gently at first, and a bit higher when he proved he could stay on. Finally, he scuffed his feet in the dirt, effectively stopping the swing. "Well, at least he's got that right," she muttered softly with a wry twist of her lips. He turned to look at her, offering a wide smile, before he ran off to one of the slides.

"Looks like you've been deserted," came a voice close to her ear.

"Yup, seems that way," she said somewhat wistfully. The little boy's straight blond hair had unexpectedly reminded her of Drew.

"Ready to go?" Drew's voice dispelled the enchantment.

"Lead on."

Fifteen minutes later, Drew pulled up before Stacy's home.

"Wow, what a day," she said.

He switched off the ignition and turned to look at her. "I'm glad it worked out."

Stacy, affected by the disturbing expression in his eyes, decided to steer toward safer waters. "I like your mother."

"Most people do."

"Well"—she lowered her lashes—"I'd better be getting in, or Dad will wonder what's keeping me."

As she started up the stairs she heard his firm footsteps right behind her. But then her attention was caught by the sound of the telephone ringing inside the apartment. She ran up the rest of the stairs, fumbled with the key in the lock, and pushed open the door.

Sprinting to the kitchen phone, she grabbed it and, drawing a deep breath, she said, "Hello. Davidson residence."

"May I speak to Mr. Pitman?" The feminine voice on the line was elusively familiar, and for a second Stacy feared it was Jennifer. She was still trying to place the voice as she handed the phone to Drew. "It's for you."

While he listened to the caller, Stacy, restless, got a glass out of the cupboard, filled it with ice and tap water. She heard the ice cracking and, trying not to eavesdrop on Drew's side of the conversation, she focused her concentration on the glass, swishing the cubes around and then sipping the cooled liquid.

After hanging up, Drew came over and stood before her. Stacy looked up and noticed his grim expression.

"Where's your liquor?"

A little shocked, Stacy mutely pointed and stood unmoving as he found a bottle and then searched until he located the glasses. He poured a bit in the bottom of a glass and handed it to her. "Drink this," he ordered.

"What?"

"Drink." She obeyed, realizing he wasn't going to offer any explanation until she had complied.

She grimaced after she swallowed the bitter spirits. "Now, tell me what this is about."

"That was Muriel Goodwin on the phone."

Her mind fit the piece in place and she said intuitively, "Has something happened to Dad?" She watched Drew hesitate. "Please . . . tell me!"

"He's had a heart attack."

"Oh, my God!"

Drew's hands shot out and supported her slumping body against his chest. "He's alive and under his doctor's care at the hospital."

"I've got to go to him." Her voice was little short of a wail.

"I'll drive you. You've got to pull yourself together. You can't see him like this." His voice was a firm command.

She took in a shuddering breath and, pushing away from him, said steadily, "Okay. I'm ready."

He surveyed her quickly. Then, taking her by the arm, they rushed out into the twilight.

Stacy never remembered much about the journey to the hospital. Stunned, she sat there whispering over and over to herself a prayer for help. Once they arrived, Drew took charge, and he led her through the maze of corridors.

Stacy felt cold, numb, chilled by the sterile, antiseptic hospital smells. Muriel and Katie were already there in the intensive-care waiting room when they arrived.

Stacy felt herself enfolded by Muriel. "I'm so sorry

this happened. The doctor just told us that his condition has stabilized. Each minute he holds on improves his chances."

Standing back, Stacy quietly wiped her tears away before asking, "What happened? He was so chipper this morning."

"Your father's been under a lot of stress lately. His blood pressure has been way up, but he didn't want to worry you. I guess he just did too much."

"I've warned him about taking it easy—oh, why didn't he listen! I should have watched him better."

"Now, Stacy, you can't blame yourself. He's a grown man."

Stacy started to weep again and Drew guided her over to a sofa. Pressing her face against his shoulder, he held her securely, stroking her back.

At last she raised her head and he wiped the tears away with his handkerchief. Stacy gazed into his eyes, indescribably comforted by his silent understanding.

She saw him glance up at someone behind her and she twisted around. There stood Dr. MacIntyre, their family physician.

Reading the mute question in her eyes, he said, "He's doing as well as can be expected. Is this your fiancé?" At her nod, he continued: "Good. Your father specifically asked to see you both."

They followed him down the long, pale green corridor. Just before he pushed open the heavy door, Dr. MacIntyre warned her, "Don't be frightened by the equipment. It's all part of the monitoring system. I don't want you to stay more than five minutes, and whatever you do, don't upset him. You'll have to be brave. . . . Ready?"

"Yes, Doctor." She lifted her chin and tried to smile.

"Okay." He held open the door for them to pass through and then led the way over to her father's bed.

Drew squeezed her hand, but she could not look at him. All she could do was stare at the strange sight of her father lying so still in the bed and the bewildering assortment of machines. Drew spoke first. "Hi, Bob." His voice was easy, his mouth curled in a smile. "Seems to me you're trying awfully hard to skip out on some work."

Bob smiled wanly. "Drew . . . thank God you're here."

"Hi, Daddy." Stacy kissed his pale cheek.

"Hi . . . kitten."

She smiled, blinking back the tears that threatened to overflow. "Daddy, you don't need to talk."

"Rest easier . . . knowing you're taking care of her, Drew." His eyes pierced the younger man.

"Glad to do it." He slipped his arm around Stacy's waist and gazed down at her, then back to Bob. "By the way, you'll be happy to hear we've set the date for the wedding."

Stacy smothered a gasp and, looking at her father, saw the stricken man's spirits visibly lighten. "Good. . . . When?"

"Four weeks from today."

"I'll be there . . . need to give the bride away."

"Right."

"You have to leave now. Bob should rest." Dr. MacIntyre's voice sounded behind them.

"Bye, Daddy. Sleep well." She bent to kiss his gaunt cheek once more before turning away from the bed.

Dr. MacIntyre came out behind them. "It should be just a matter of time before he's home. He suffered minor damage to his heart, but if he clears the next forty-eight hours, the prognosis is excellent."

"Is there anything we can do?" The anxiety was clear in her tone.

"No, but your news helped. It gave him something to

hang on to. Convalescence isn't pleasant for a man who is used to being active. Go home now and get some rest." He inspected her shrewdly. "Do you want me to prescribe a sedative?"

"No, thanks. I'll be all right."

"Good. Now if you'll excuse me, I have several more patients to see. Good night." He shook Stacy's hand and then Drew's before walking briskly away.

Muriel stood up as they went back into the waiting room. "How's he doing?"

"As well as can be expected," Stacy replied, repeating the doctor's words. "We spoke with him for a few minutes."

"I'll bet that made him feel better. He's been so anxious about you. While we waited for the ambulance he talked of you."

Overcome, tears choked Stacy's throat. Drew said, "I think I set his mind at rest. In four weeks Stacy becomes my wife."

"Oh, how nice!" Muriel exclaimed. "I'm sure that pleased him."

"You can find out for yourself when you visit him," Drew told her.

"Oh, I think they're only allowing the immediate family to see him." She spoke levelly, but her eyes gave her away.

"I'll speak to Dr. MacIntyre," Drew said. "He might make an exception for you. Bob's health is what's important, and to see you would be good for him."

"Thank you. I'd like to see him." Then, turning her attention to Stacy, she said, "Why don't you stay with us tonight?"

Stacy sighed. "That's very nice of you."

"Not at all. Drew can drive you home to pick up a few things and I'll inform the nurses' station where you'll be." Muriel did not need to explain why the hospital might want to get in touch.

"We'll meet you there in about an hour," Drew said, and he and Stacy left.

When they were in the relative privacy of the car, Stacy confronted Drew. "Why did you lie to my father?"

"You heard the doctor. Your father shouldn't be worried about anything, and your future was obviously preying on his mind."

His tone was persuasive, his logic irrefutable, but Stacy objected. "But to lie so blatantly . . ."

"Who says it's a lie? We're getting married in four weeks."

Stacy gasped. His face was shadowed and she couldn't read the expression in his eyes. "You must be kidding. If this is your idea of a joke . . ."

"Not at all. I've told him we're getting married, and we are."

"What if I don't go along with it?"

Even in the dim light she saw him quirk one eyebrow. "You will to please your father. You won't risk another heart attack by calling it off." Then he set the car in motion, terminating the discussion.

As they drove, Stacy wondered about the repercussions of tonight's announcement. She felt cornered. First, there were her father's expectations and the subsequent effect on his health; and then there was Drew's presumptive attitude. Added to this was the knowledge that she loved him! Under other circumstances if he had asked her to marry him, she would be bursting with happiness. But she did not understand what his motives were. He didn't profess to love her, and he hadn't known her father very long. Why did he want to marry her?

She tackled him on that score as soon as they were back in her living room.

"Would you explain to me why you want to get married? What's in this for you? Just a few weeks ago you claimed the engagement was a cover to avoid marriage." She couldn't bring herself to utter Jennifer's name.

She thought she detected a spasm of pain in his eyes, but it was gone in an instant and he said calmly, "Well, quite frankly, I've gotten used to the idea; I want a settled home." He continued dispassionately: "Plus both our parents are in favor. You'd make a good wife for a man in my position. You've grown up with this kind of work and know the score."

All good reasons, she thought in anguish, but what about love? Where does that fit in?

He raised his hand and gently brushed a few strands of her hair back and then stroked her cheek, mesmerizing her with his eyes.

"Stacy, will you marry me?"

She blinked, and then, dropping her lashes, she hesitated, irresolute. Bleakly, she realized her life would be empty without him. *So what if he doesn't love me? I love him! And somehow I'll break down that wall he's built around his emotions.*

She glanced back up and saw him watching, waiting for her answer. Surrendering to her heart's desire, she said, "Yes."

"Good! Let's seal the bargain."

He surrounded her with his arms, pulling her up against his lean body, and bent his head to deeply kiss her parted lips.

Lured on by his tantalizing touch, Stacy gave herself up to the pleasure of his possession. She felt the warmth of his body beneath her palms. And, as he pressed her closer to his thighs, she slid one hand up over his shoulder to the back of his head, twining her fingers through his thick, silky hair.

Slowly, he released her mouth and gazed into her eyes as if searching for something. Then, with a wry twist to his lips, he said, "We've got a lot going for us."

Chilled by the cool self-possession in his voice, Stacy found herself at a loss for words. She wanted nothing more than to tell him that she loved him, but pride stayed her voice. She could not make such a confession while he sounded so detached.

Lifting his wrist, he glanced at his watch. "We need to get a move on. The Goodwins are waiting up for you." With his hands on her shoulders, he turned her around to the doorway, gave her a slight push, and playfully slapped her bottom. "Hurry up and pack."

"It won't take five minutes," she tossed back over her shoulder.

She'd follow his lead and play it cool . . . no fervent exchange of intimacies . . . no passionate avowal of love . . .

Chapter Nine

The morning of the ceremony dawned cool, grey, and overcast; and it had not improved by the time Stacy was ready to drive over to the Goodwins' house to change for the wedding. As she drove she mentally recounted the events of the intervening weeks.

With less than a month to organize everything, Stacy had been caught up in a tidal wave of activities. For the first eight days she had spent much of her time visiting her father; but as he continued to make strong progress, she had allowed her emphasis to shift to the preparations for the wedding and reception.

Muriel Goodwin had been a life-saver, lending her support during the early days of her father's illness and then donating her time and energy to assist the young bride.

Originally, Stacy had taken an extended leave of absence from work; later, after her father informed her of his intention to take an early retirement, with consulting work to keep him involved on a small scale, she decided to resign. She had enjoyed working in the oil business, but with her father no longer in the office she preferred to make a clean break and find another position once her life had returned to a steadier pace.

As Stacy drove closer to the Goodwins' she was compelled to use the windshield wipers as the clouds opened up. The weather matched her mood, her optimism having drained away as her nuptials approached. The wipers' steady beat sounded like the ticking of a clock, ticking away her final minutes of freedom.

Although she had seen Drew during the past few weeks, dates and visits to the hospital, not since she had agreed to marry him had he displayed more than a modicum of affection. Concluding that he felt trapped and wanted to back out of his commitment, but was too proud to call it off, Stacy had decided to confront him after he brought her home from the rehearsal dinner.

First she had offered him a drink, and when he was comfortably settled on the sofa she had remained standing, restless, uncertain how to begin. Finally, with a quick sip of her own drink, she said disjointedly, "Are . . . are you sure you want to go through with the ceremony?"

Drew regarded her agitated movements with amusement and answered, "Quite sure—you aren't suggesting that we live together, are you?"

She twisted around and stared at him in amazement. "No! Certainly not!"

He snapped his fingers. "Then I guess I'll have to marry you."

"Oh, stop it! This is no time for jokes. . . . What I want to say is"—she took a breath and plunged on—"my father is much better. He could handle it if we told him the wedding is off."

"But I don't want to do that." She saw him smile. "No one is holding a gun to my back."

"Ohhhh . . . how can you sit there so calmly!"

"One of us has to be." His voice was unperturbed. "I've made my decision and I'm standing by it. You've just got pre-wedding nerves. Quit being so jittery and come sit down." His words were pleasant enough, but Stacy sensed their underlying edge of steel. He touched the cushion next to him and she found herself weakly obeying. He set his drink down on the coffee table and placed hers alongside. Then he leaned back facing her, resting his arm on the back of the sofa, his fingers gently twisting a tendril of her hair.

"Look at me," he commanded, and she gazed at him, slightly disconcerted by his light touch on her hair. "You've been under a lot of strain. Just relax and take things as they come. We're getting married tomorrow, and then we'll drive over to San Antonio for a few days."

His voice soothed her slightly, but she searched his rugged features, trying in vain to discover some sign that he truly cared. Sighing deeply, she turned away and stared unseeingly across the room.

"Stacy . . . Stacy!" He tugged on the strands of hair he had wound around his fingers. She glanced back at him, noting that the muscles in his jaw were set. His blue eyes bore into her. "We've made a commitment; you are going to be my wife."

Chilled by his tone, she opened her mouth to protest, but with a lightning movement he was leaning over, pressing her mouth with his, in a kiss which told her more than words alone of his inflexible determination.

As he raised his head, his mouth tilted into a smile.

"Don't worry. I'll see you at two tomorrow." With a tap on her cheek, he quietly rose to his feet and without waiting for her to see him out, he strode away, leaving her alone and more confused then ever.

Why am I so miserable? she asked herself. But she did not need an answer; she knew what it was; three little words would have changed everything.

The blast of the car horn behind her snapped her out of her reverie. The light at which she had stopped was now green. Releasing her foot from the brake, the car lurched forward, almost stalling. Quickly she focused her attention on the automobile and pressed down on the accelerator. Casting a glance in the rearview mirror, Stacy saw the digruntled male driver mutter and shake his head.

Her lips lifted into a smile. "He's probably cursing women drivers," she murmured to herself. "Oh, well, you can't win them all."

Her concentration once more on driving, it was several seconds before she perceived that the rain had ceased and now the sun was breaking through the clouds in glorious rays, shimmering off the wet pavement.

Inexplicably, her mood lightened.

As though they had been watching for her, the Goodwins' front door opened as Stacy came up the front walk. Although Katie and Muriel were standing at the threshold wearing robes, the rest of their appearance indicated they needed only to don their dresses.

Both women hugged her before they took her upstairs to the bedroom which they had prepared for her use. Stacy's wedding gown was laid out on the double bed, and Katie, as maid of honor, insisted on waiting on her.

"I have to make myself useful somehow. You and Mom have taken care of everything else."

"It was very generous of her to help." Stacy considered herself very lucky to have such kind friends. Had her mother been alive, the tasks would have rested on her shoulders, but since she wasn't, Stacy was happy to have Muriel's assistance.

"She was glad to do it," Katie told her. "Besides, it gets her in practice for my turn."

"Is that a hint?" Stacy asked.

"Oh, no . . . I'm not ready to get married."

"You're the same age as I am."

"Yes, but you found the right man," Katie pointed out. And Stacy's eyes clouded over with doubt while Katie continued teasingly: "I must confess—it makes me jealous every time Drew looks at you."

"Huh . . . ? What are you talking about?"

Katie paused and then she vaguely waved the comb which she was using to work Stacy's long hair into curls at the crown of her head. "It's just something that shines in his eyes . . . pride or love or something. . . ." Her voice drifted off, slightly embarrassed.

"Or the gleam of male superiority," Stacy quipped.

But Katie's observation gave her food for thought until her friend said: "I think your hair looks terrific— even if I do say so myself."

Stacy gazed into the dressing table mirror. "You have done a wonderful job. Thank you." She twisted around on the stool and hugged Katie, who beamed with pleasure at her praise.

"Well, it's about time you dressed."

Stacy noted the time on the bedside clock and, agreeing, she walked over to the bed.

Muriel, now arrayed in a plum-colored georgette dress, came in while Katie fastened the long row of buttons up the back of the gown. She clasped her hands together and said, "Every bride is beautiful, Stacy, but today you outshine them all."

Smiling her thanks, she stared at her reflection, not quite able to believe it was she. The delicate ecru lace hugged her throat and shoulders and formed graceful bell sleeves whose scalloped edges draped over her wrists. As she twisted to see the back, the lace train floated out behind her, giving her an ethereal feeling. Creamy silk lined the gown from the bodice to the hem.

Carefully, Muriel picked up the antique veil and set it on Stacy's hair. "This is such a lovely veil." She stepped back to admire the net and lace confection.

"My grandmother was the first bride to wear it, then Mother." Stacy's voice faded and she finished softly, "Now it's my turn."

"I'm sure you'll be as lucky as they were," Muriel predicted.

Stacy could not speak. Memories of her parents flashed through her mind. She had had a warm, loving childhood, growing up surrounded by the security of two devoted people. Suddenly, it came to her that Drew had not experienced such a home life. He had grown up emotionally starved for affection and had bravely concealed it behind a thick crust of independence and self-confidence. Intuitively, she was convinced that this was the key. Without the day-to-day experience of love in his life, he had never learned its true meaning.

With a resurgence of optimism, Stacy thought that if she demonstrated to Drew the power of love he would eventually understand it and one day . . . reciprocate it. Passion and sex had their roles in a marriage, but without love it was a hollow shell. Hope radiated through her, sparkling her eyes, and lightening her heart.

Peering through the netting, Stacy watched as the last guests and Drew's mother were seated. Then the organ swelled into the ageless measures of the wedding march. Katie was her only attendant. Stacy had wanted to keep the arrangements simple, but they had mushroomed until there were over one hundred guests standing awaiting the bride.

Her father's eyes rested on her proudly and she smiled back as she tucked her hand around his arm. As she stepped down the aisle her brown eyes scanned the sea of friendly faces until they reached Drew. He stood at the base of the steps leading to the altar. Next to him was his best man, Jim Foster, a friend from his college days. Stacy thought Jim appeared more nervous than the groom, who held himself with dignity, a slight smile curving his lips.

A tremor passed through her as Drew received her from her father. Unsteady, she cautiously ascended the steps to the minister.

Listening to the sacred words, the scent of her bouquet floated up to her, mingled with the smell of burning candles and Drew's elusive cologne. She fixed her eyes on the strong brown hands which held hers while Drew and then she repeated their vows. As he slipped the gold band on her finger, she raised her lashes and was vaguely comforted by his reassuring smile.

Katie had to nudge her before Stacy remembered to get Drew's ring. A little flustered and with hands which shook slightly, she slid it onto his finger.

After the minister's final words, Drew hesitated an instant, staring deeply into her eyes before he raised her veil and bestowed the sealing kiss. His mouth lingered on hers and her heart missed a beat.

In the narthex, they paused to sign the license and

then they were surrounded by their friends. After a few minutes of chaotic greetings, Drew grasped her arm and guided her to the waiting limousine which would convey them to the reception at a downtown hotel.

Alone with Drew, Stacy could think of nothing to say. Several strained minutes had passed when Drew broke the silence. "That wasn't so bad, was it?" he asked drolly.

"No. It went smoothly." Stacy was surprised that her voice sounded so normal. Then she found herself confessing, "I'm glad I didn't trip."

He chuckled. "I pity anyone who that happens to."

They continued talking lightly about unimportant topics for the remainder of the journey, but with part of her mind Stacy wondered at Drew's casualness.

The reception was very exhilarating. So many toasts were given that Stacy was lightheaded by the time Katie helped her to change into her emerald-green traveling suit.

With forced cheerfulness she hugged her father and kissed his cheek before Drew tucked her hand into the crook of his arm and led her through the gauntlet of well-wishers scattering rice and rose petals across their heads and shoulders.

The black paint of Drew's car was barely recognizable for all the slogans decorating it. Her tension momentarily forgotten, Stacy laughed as they drove away, the sound of dozens of tin cans drowning out the throbbing engine. Drew threw her a surprised glance and then his deep chuckle blended with hers.

After he drove for several blocks, he pulled the car over, uncoiled his long length, and climbed out. When he returned he tossed several strings of cans to the back of the car. "It must have taken weeks to collect those."

Stacy giggled at his mock stern expression, and he regarded her closely. "You enjoyed the champagne?"

"Of course. . . . It was delightful."

Shaking his head in amusement, he grinned. "You're tipsy."

"No . . . I . . . am . . . not." She carefully enunciated the words; her tongue suddenly seemed too big for her mouth.

"Whatever you say," he teased.

Stacy rested her head against the seat and closed her eyes to blot out the spinning images. Much to her disgust, she admitted to herself that her stomach felt decidedly queasy. She was sorry now that she hadn't eaten more of the canapés or finger sandwiches which had been served at the reception. *All I need is to be sick!* she thought wryly. She opened her eyes and gazed out the window in an effort to divert her mind from her churning insides. The daylight was already fading as they sped down the highway to San Antonio.

Drew seemed disinclined to talk and switched on the tape player. Immediately, the soothing music of *Swan Lake* filled the car and Stacy found her senses lulled.

When the automobile halted, Stacy raised her lids, slowly, vaguely aware that she must have dozed off. Her forehead was resting on Drew's jacket sleeve. She peeked up at him through her lashes and encountered his amused expression. Sitting up smartly, she smoothed her skirt and fingered her hair.

"You look fine," Drew told her. "After we check in I'll buy you dinner."

"Good. I didn't eat very much today."

"Really?"

Stacy scowled at him.

In response he leaned over and kissed her provocative mouth. As he sat back he observed, "That's better. You don't look so much like an impudent schoolgirl."

Bristling, Stacy waited mutely until Drew came

around and helped her out. Then still holding her hand, they walked into the bustling hotel lobby.

As they made their way to the bridal suite, Stacy forced her lagging steps to keep pace with Drew's easy strides. The rooms were opulently decorated with a thick pile carpet and reproductions of English Georgian furniture. Standing in the middle of the lounge, Stacy watched through the open bedroom doorway as the bellboy deposited their bags on luggage racks. Then her eye was drawn to the huge bed draped with a gold satin spread. Identical fabric covered the padded headboard and hung from a cornice on the wall behind the bed. The sumptuous effect harkened back to a bygone age when life was more ostentatious.

"Oh, my," Stacy whispered aloud to herself, "what have I let myself in for?" Tonight there would be no barriers to Drew's passionate possession. Suddenly Stacy was assailed by a feeling of bitter-sweetness: bitter to be claimed by a man who did not love her; sweet to explore the hidden depths of passion with a man whose lightest touch sparked her deepest longings.

Brusquely, Drew tipped the departing bellboy. "Let's get ready for dinner. I'm starving."

"Shouldn't we unpack?" Stacy found herself suggesting, and at the same time wondering if she was trying to prolong the inevitable.

"Don't bother. The maid will do it while we're at dinner."

"Okay. I'll just wash my hands," she said.

Stacy opened two closet doors before she found the one leading into the bathroom. It was fitted with a sunken marble tub and the walls were covered with etched mirrors.

Blushing at her disturbing visions, she quickly steered her thoughts to the task at hand. Using a brush from her purse, she smoothed back her hair and with the puff from her compact she powdered her shiny nose. She didn't need any color on her cheeks, she noted; they were already bright pink. Taking a deep breath, she snapped her bag closed and rejoined Drew.

The hotel's dining room, like the rest of its facilities, was first class. While they lingered over their dinner of beef stroganoff, Stacy prudently sipped only a small quantity of the dry wine which accompanied their meal.

After his plate was removed, Drew pushed away from the table and said, "Why don't we take a walk down by the river? I need to work off this dinner."

Unaccountably, Stacy smarted under his prosaic tone. Instead of sounding like an eager bridegroom, he seemed more suited to the role of an inveterate husband. Miffed, she agreed tersely.

Outside they followed the street for a ways and then descended a flight of steps which led to San Antonio's famous river walk. Even at this late hour there were crowds of people, and the path was well lit with strings of lights, so even though the sky had clouded over they could see clearly. Spicy scents from the sidewalk cafés blended with the smell of the river and trees.

Stacy figured that they must have walked about a mile when Drew finally suggested that they retrace their steps. Her feet were aching by the time they had reached the intimate privacy of their room. She thought ruefully that if she had known they were going to spend the evening strolling around, she would have worn appropriate footwear. All she wanted to do was kick off her shoes and soak her feet in some hot water.

Drew's voice interrupted her musings. "Why don't you use the bathroom first? I haven't read today's paper yet." His hand indicated the newspaper and magazines arranged neatly on a low table.

"Fine," she agreed, confused once again by his remote demeanor. She had not expected him to pounce on her once they were alone, but this was ridiculous!

She opted for a warm shower, and after she had toweled dry she slipped on the silky white peignoir which she had bought especially for this night.

Drew was still scanning the paper when she re-entered the lounge. He had removed his jacket and tie, but otherwise had not bothered to change.

He glanced up and saw her hesitating just inside the doorway. For a moment Stacy thought she glimpsed a kindling of hunger in his eyes; then they were veiled by his lashes and he briskly folded the paper and tossed it to a table as he stood up. Without another look in her direction, he walked through the doorway, saying over his shoulder, "I'll take my turn now."

Flummoxed, Stacy paced across the room, growing angrier with each step. She didn't know what he was trying to prove; whatever it was, she did not like it. She thought back over the preceding weeks, recalling that except for an occasional kiss, Drew had rarely touched her.

By the time he returned, wearing pajama bottoms and a robe, Stacy had worked herself into a flaming temper.

"That wasn't long," she said sharply.

He glanced at her, perplexed. "No, it wasn't."

"I'm surprised you didn't drag it out."

He raised his brow. "You don't sound much like a timid maiden." His voice sounded sardonic.

"How am I supposed to react when you make your disinterest so blatant?"

"Is that the problem?" Stacy should have been wary of the iron ring in his voice, but she was beyond discretion. "You've hardly looked at me all evening, and then you . . . you read the paper!" She gestured dramatically at the innocent newsprint.

"I'm looking at you now—come here."

"Why should I?" she answered, oblivious to his cold, intimidating gaze.

"Because you're my wife."

"Big deal!" She had not meant those words to slip out. Uneasily, she ran the tip of her tongue along her lips. His face became thunderous and automatically she stepped back a pace.

Swiftly, he crossed the intervening space and grasped her tightly, his fingers digging into her arms. "Don't you move away from me!" he blurted out.

Although she tried to pull away, his hold was too strong. "Let me go!"

"No! You're my wife. I can do practically anything I want." His jaw clenched.

She continued to argue: "This is the twentieth century . . . I have rights!"

"Oh, really," he drawled menacingly. "So do I."

"A husband can't force his wife!" *Now why did I say that?* she wondered miserably. Nothing was going the way she had expected.

"I've proved on more then one occasion that I needn't use coercion." He ran his hand up across the silky fabric, over her shoulder to her neck. Uncontrollably, she trembled; her heart was pounding. He smiled smugly as his eyes flickered over her. "You are ready and . . . willing."

"My—you're so chivalrous." Her voice was scornful.

"I've never claimed to be . . . I take what I want," he told her as one hand twisted through her hair and he held her head securely as he lowered his mouth to ravage her lips.

Uselessly she struggled against his insolent possession, pummeling his solid back with her fists. He grabbed her flaying hands and pinned them to her sides by wrapping one long arm around her slender body and grasping the opposite wrist. Effectively bound, gagging her vocal protests with his mouth, he brazenly moved his other hand over the curves of her hips, up past her waist until it closed over her breast. Dextrously, he kneaded the swelling tissue until the tip hardened.

He raised his head, arrogantly staring into her eyes. Stacy's breathing was rapid and shallow as she tried to control her betraying responses.

"So much for your objections," he said.

"You beast!" she hissed through clenched teeth.

"You say one thing, but your body tells a different story."

Then, unexpectedly, she burst into tears.

He muttered an oath and contemptuously flung her away. Frantically, she grabbed the back of a chair for support.

"Spare me the tears." His gruff voice sounded disgusted. "Go to bed. I won't bother you again." Stacy watched through stricken eyes as he turned on his heel and paced over to the built-in bar, flinging open doors until he located a glass and bottle. He lifted his proud head and glared at her. "Get out of my sight!"

Biting back a sharp retort, she straightened away from the chair, regarding him wide-eyed. And then she dashed into the bedroom, slammed the door, and flung herself on the bed, burying her face in the cool, soft pillow, weeping bitterly over the fiasco which she had created.

At some point she must have fallen asleep, because the next thing she knew it was morning and the sun was blazing through the undrawn drapes. She rolled onto her back, staring up at the ceiling and bleakly reflecting on last night's disaster.

She realized, belatedly, she had misjudged Drew's motives. Thinking clearer this morning, she discerned that originally he had tried to relieve the inherent tension by not pressing her. Unfortunately, her frayed nerves had misconstrued this as indifference.

Dispiritedly, she slid off the bed and went into the bathroom to bathe her puffy eyelids with cool water.

"Well, my girl, you really blew it this time," she said to her mirror image. "What are you going to do?"

"I'll tell you." Stacy jumped, startled by the sound of Drew's voice, and she stared at the reflection looming behind hers. His eyes were bloodshot and his chin was shadowed by his beard. He was naked from the waist up. By his disreputable appearance she assumed he had not spent a peaceful night. While she was absorbing these impressions, he continued: "First we're going down to breakfast. Then we'll go out sightseeing."

"Sounds good." She managed to keep her words steady. "I've finished in here—I'll go get dressed."

He nodded in agreement and she slipped around him and out the door.

Minutes later she had applied a light cover of makeup and had zipped up her dirndl skirt and was reaching for her print blouse when he appeared and leaned against the wall, his arms folded across his chest.

Quickly she thrust her arms into the full sleeves, conscious of his disturbing presence. When the last button was fastened, she turned to him.

Giving her a lopsided grin, he said, "My head is pounding. Do you have any aspirin?"

"Yes, in my tote bag." She rummaged through the contents of the bag while he waited. Out of the corner of her eye she saw him yawn and stretch, the muscles of his chest rippling under the mat of hair and his pajamas loosely clinging to his lean hips.

With a groan he clutched his head. "Something tells me last night didn't work out very well."

Stacy looked up curiously. "Don't you remember?" she asked.

"Not much," he said with a rueful grin. "Fill me in."

Unsure of what to say, she paused, thinking swiftly. "What's the last thing you recall?"

"We went for a walk by the river—didn't we?"

"Yes."

"That's it." His eyes locked with hers.

Stacy released her breath slowly. "I think the combination of champagne and wine got to you. You went into the lounge while I changed. . . . I guess you must have passed out." Deliberately, she skipped several major points.

"How about you?"

"I fell asleep on the bed." She indicated the rumpled sheets.

Shrewdly, he stared at her, but her carefully schooled expression gave nothing away. He shrugged his shoulders as if dismissing it, took the bottle of aspirin from her, and went into the bathroom.

"He really doesn't remember!" she whispered to herself. She had been so worried about facing him this morning, and now, like a gift from heaven, the memory of that sordid argument had been wiped away.

Shaking her head in amazement, she walked out to the lounge. She halted, spotting the half-empty bottle. Furtively, she cleared it away. She would not leave anything to joggle his memory. Then her eyes inspected the room, and with a spark of amusement she set to work returning the sofa to its normal condition, fluffing the pillows and smoothing the fabric.

"Well," she mused to herself while she straightened up, "this honeymoon isn't quite as I'd envisioned, but I'm not going to rock the boat."

During the subsequent days Drew and Stacy spent their time on companionable outings, revisiting such well-known landmarks as the Alamo, which they now viewed with an adult perspective and understanding of the brave men who lost their lives there. One evening they went to the dinner theater, and for another Drew persuaded Stacy to go to a pro-basketball game.

Each night when they returned to their hotel suite, Drew's manner became distant and withdrawn. And he always chose to sleep on the lounge sofa, leaving Stacy alone in the vast bed.

When Stacy was besieged by doubts, she firmly suppressed them and took each day as it came, content, at least temporarily, with Drew's friendly company. She knew that this unnatural situation could not last indefinitely, but she was too proud to make the first overture, and remembering how ineptly she had handled their wedding night, she forebore provoking any confrontation. It had been like igniting a fuse to a stick of dynamite, and the memory of the resulting explosion still sent shivers down her spine.

Chapter Ten

One morning, a few days after Stacy had settled into her new home, she dismally surveyed the kitchen. *What this place needs,* she told herself, *is a fresh coat of paint.* Although Drew had suggested that she might make changes in the decor, she had confined her activities to rearranging furniture and purchasing a few knick-knacks to give it a homier atmosphere. With time on her hands, she found her purse and went out to the hardware store.

She returned an hour later with two gallons of yellow paint and all the paraphernalia she needed for the job. Around three o'clock she paused to fix a sandwich, and was contentedly munching away, admiring her work, when the phone rang.

She reached it on the second ring. "Hello."

"Hi, Stacy . . . just wanted you to know I can't make it back for dinner," Drew said.

"Oh?" In spite of herself she was plagued by doubts. Drew was a virile man, and she realized that if he did not satisfy his masculine needs with his wife, then he might choose to seek satisfaction elsewhere.

"Yes. I'm meeting several men from United Oil. I'll be in late, so you don't have to wait up for me."

"Of course not," she said, chagrined. *Why bother waiting up for a husband who sleeps in a separate bedroom?* she thought grimly. A dismal feeling swept over her.

"Why don't you invite Katie over?" Drew's voice suggested.

"I can't do that. The place is at sixes and sevens. By the time I get it cleaned up it will be too late."

"What are you doing?" His tone was mildly curious.

"Nothing much," she told him. "I'm painting the kitchen."

"You should have hired someone."

She sighed despondently and found herself explaining, "Since I haven't found a new job, I have plenty of time."

"Okay, I'll let you get back to it. Bye, Stacy."

"Bye, Drew," she responded just as the line went dead.

Briskly she straightened up the debris from her sparse lunch and returned to work. The task took much longer then she had anticipated since she decided to go ahead and apply a second coat after Drew's phone call. By the time she had restored the kitchen to its former order, it was past seven. She was tired, but her stomach growled with hunger so she heated and consumed a small can of stew before she went upstairs to bathe.

Splatters of paint covered her arms and legs, and it took quite a while for her to effectively clean all of the spots with turpentine. After using the smelly solution, she decided that she needed a bath more than ever.

Slowly she eased her body into the tub filled with rich fragrant bubble bath and relaxed with her eyes closing from weariness. The water had cooled and she was preparing to emerge when the door opened and Drew strolled in. Barely daring to breathe, she plunged her body beneath the water, but little foam remained to protect her modesty. She blushed hotly as Drew slowly scrutinized her appearance and said sharply, "So here you are."

Stacy wondered at the note of concern in his voice. Peeking up at him, she detected a strange glint in his eyes.

"Didn't you hear me call?"

"No." She nodded in the direction of the door. "It was closed."

He continued to stare. "Have you just recently finished painting?"

"Yes. It took most of the day. . . . I thought you were going to be home late," she answered.

"We got done early." He leaned casually against the doorjamb, his arms folded across his chest as though he had all the time in the world to chat. Stacy wished he would leave. Between the tepid water and the draft from the open doorway, she was becoming quite cold and had to clamp her teeth together to keep them from chattering.

"I've been through the kitchen. You did an excellent job."

High praise, indeed! she thought to herself. Aloud, she said, "Th-thank you."

"You look ready to turn blue," he observed with a faint smile. "Come on, get out of that tub."

"Not until you go," she snapped.

Ignoring her request, he stepped forward, grabbing a towel off the rack. "Stand up!" he ordered implacably.

Reluctantly, she obeyed, crossing her arms in front of

her body. She could not meet his eyes. He might be her husband, but this was the first time he had seen her totally nude. Spreading the towel out as if to wrap it around her, Drew paused, running his eyes over her smooth skin, drinking in her loveliness like a parched man.

"My God, you're beautiful," he murmured as he enfolded her in the fluffy fabric and rubbed her dry. By the time he was done she felt comfortably warm; her nerve endings were tingling from his intimate touch. As if compelled by some force stronger then herself, Stacy raised her lashes. Her breath caught in her throat at the passionate desire glowing in his eyes.

Frightened by his smoldering gaze, Stacy took a ragged breath and tried to side-step around him. He anticipated her move and she plunged against the wall of his chest as he plucked the towel from her nerveless grasp. Flinging it aside, he imprisoned her body against his. "I've waited too long," he muttered just as his lips came down on hers in a searing kiss.

She tore her mouth away and said, her voice faltering, "I . . . I'm not ready." But deep in her soul a voice whispered, *Liar!*

"Yes, you are," he said hoarsely. "Your body is on fire." He traced a finger sensuously over her flesh. Then with a slow, deliberate move he cupped her chin and forced her head up to meet his demanding mouth.

As she quivered against him the pressure of his warm lips softened into a tantalizing caress. His tongue gently probed her lips apart. Her resistance ebbed away, dissolved by his ardent exploration.

Sensing her capitulation, Drew swung her up in his arms and carried her through to the bedroom, never allowing her to re-establish her defenses by continuing his seductive stroking of her breast with the tips of his calloused fingers and teasing the bare skin of her shoulder and throat with titillating kisses.

He set her on her feet for an instant while he threw back the bed covers, and then he was lowering her to the bed, pushing her back onto the soft cotton sheets and covering her body with his.

The buttons of his shirt pressed into her tender skin, but after kissing her for another moment he uttered a muffled groan, rolled off the bed, and stood up, jerking his shirt from the waistband as he unfastened it. Quickly he shrugged out of the sleeves and Stacy watched transfixed as he continued to undress.

Any niggling doubts were overpowered by the love that welled up inside her. She knew that this was the moment that she had been craving. It was right for him to possess her completely.

Instinctively, with a naturally seductive movement, she raised her arms to him as he stepped out of his clothes. He melted his powerful body against her and her nostrils caught his distinctive masculine scent. His hardening muscles mutely proclaimed his desire. Gently teasing her with his hands and mouth, he patiently continued to arouse her with infinite care until she reached a fevered pitch. She felt as though she'd go mad unless he filled the gnawing void deep within her. Sensing her readiness, he rained fervent kisses on her mouth. Caught up in a vortex of sensual delight, Stacy arched her back to meet his movements until all her senses exploded with ultimate fulfillment.

During the night, half-asleep, Stacy stretched her legs against the uncomfortably binding sheets.

"Stacy? You awake?" came a deep voice from out of the darkness.

"Hmm?"

"Quit kicking me!"

Her lids flew open as the masculine sound penetrated her consciousness. "Drew?"

"Yes?"

Instantly the events of the night flooded back into her mind and with a start she realized that what she had thought were sheets were actually his long legs.

Embarrassed, she shifted away.

"Where are you going?" Drew asked.

"Nowhere . . . I'm just trying to get comfortable." Her voice quavered.

He chuckled deep in his throat. "You're not used to sleeping with a man."

Stacy was grateful for the concealing blackness as she experienced a rush of warmth to her cheeks. "Oh, really?" she responded with flippancy.

"Yes." He growled near her ear. Suddenly he moved across her, his chest covering her rosy-tipped breasts, the mat of hair tickling her sensitive skin. She could not see the expression in his eyes, but his altered breathing told its own story.

He kissed a spot behind her ear, his breath tingling the lobe, and his chin rasped against her cheek. "You know," he whispered, "I don't have anything planned for today. . . . We'll spend it together."

"Oh, you'll help me paint?"

"If we ever get out of bed," he promised before sealing her lips, once more sending her senses soaring.

When she awoke again, she automatically turned to the other side of the bed, but she was disappointed. All that remained of Drew's presence was the dented pillow and wrinkled bedding.

The smell of fresh coffee wafted up to her and Stacy concluded that Drew had gone down to fix breakfast. Smiling to herself, she got up and slipped on a robe. As she tied its belt a feeling of disquiet came over her—she could hear no sounds coming from below. Becoming uneasy, she hurried down the stairs. Her eyes scanned the living room before she continued through to the kitchen.

No one was there!

Hot tears scalded her eyes as she noticed a pot of coffee staying warm on the range. *At least I didn't imagine that!* she thought dejectedly. *Where is Drew?* Hurt that he had deserted her, it was a few minutes until she saw the note propped on the counter near the phone.

She opened the single folded sheet of paper. Her fingers were trembling.

"Dear Stacy," she read, "I had an emergency call early this morning. Back in a couple of days. Drew."

Well . . . that certainly explains everything! she fumed. No reference to where he'd be or what he'd be doing, and she realized, dispiritedly, there were no words of endearment.

Tears swam in her eyes and she pressed her hand to her mouth to control the betraying quiver of her lips. "Damn him! Damn Drew Pitman!" she muttered to the empty room and tossed the note aside. "I'm not going to sit around here all day!"

Checking the wall clock, she picked up the phone and dialed. "Katie," she said in a tight voice when the line was answered, "this is Stacy." She grimaced slightly to herself at her friend's surprise. "Can you meet me for lunch . . . ? One o'clock . . . ? Good. See you then."

She hung up and then went to the range to turn it off. She stared at the coffeepot, a sour taste in her mouth; she couldn't drink it now or later, so she poured it down the sink, rinsed the pot, and left it to drain.

When she reached the bedroom she flung off her robe and hurried into the bathroom. The spray of hot water stung her flesh, cleansing her. Vigorously she toweled dry, trying to wipe away the feel of Drew's hands. Then she slipped on her underwear, snatched a skirt and blouse from the closet, and pulled them on. As soon as she was ready she left the town house.

Stacy knew that the department stores would be closed for another hour, but she could not stay in the house any longer with last night's memories tormenting her. She drove aimlessly around the congested streets, focusing her concentration on anything but Drew and the pain that gnawed at her soul.

Finally she pulled into a shopping center and spent the next several hours strolling through the stores minutely studying displays, too dispirited to purchase anything. Eventually she came upon a book rack and bought a couple to while away the empty hours. Later, she considered getting some needlework, but she remembered with a glimmer of amusement that she still had several pieces unfinished at her father's apartment.

Katie was a few minutes late for lunch and Stacy sat listlessly over a cup of hot coffee, her shoulders slumped, but when she saw the other girl wend her way between the tables she lifted her chin and fixed a gay smile on her face.

As Katie sat down she peered at Stacy closely and said with a trace of ribald humor, "Gee, you look tired. . . . Been having too many late nights?"

"Being married is tough work," Stacy quipped.

"Uh-huh." Katie's tone was blatantly dubious.

Feigning indignation, Stacy retorted, "I'll have you know that I spent all day yesterday painting the kitchen."

"And how about last night?" Katie suggested with the indiscretion of a lifelong friend.

Blushing crimson under Katie's perceptive gaze, Stacy nonchalantly took a sip of her coffee.

Katie giggled. "It's not fair to tease, but I'm glad everything is going well," she said when she could control her mirth.

Stacy continued to smile, but what she really wanted to do was ask for some advice. Unfortunately, she could think of no way to broach the matter without giving away the entire mixed-up situation. *Who would believe it, anyway?* she thought. If nothing else, Drew's public performance had been that of a devoted lover.

The waitress came by and they both ordered a light lunch. Then Katie asked, "Have you found a new job?" Stacy shook her head and Katie continued: "Isn't it strange? Less then two months ago our positions were reversed—you were employed and I wasn't."

Was it possible that only eight weeks had passed? Stacy wondered. So much had happened! The well fire, the engagement, the wedding . . .

Katie's voice cut into her thoughts. "Maybe Drew won't want you to work. Has he said anything?"

"We haven't really discussed it yet."

"Oh, I guess you've been too busy with . . . other things." Amusement was back in her tone.

Stacy tried beaming like a happy young bride. "We've been married only a week."

"I know. That's why I was so surprised when you called today."

The waitress returned with their meals, and once they were alone again, Stacy admitted, "Drew's been called out of town."

"Oh, Stacy, I'm sorry—that must be rough."

"Well, I just needed to get out for a while. I'll be fine." To reassure Katie, she smiled.

"Sure you will. I'd like to be able to say I could do something with you this evening, but I have a date."

"Oh? With whom?" Stacy had been disgusted with

Paul's double-dealing, and he was part of the reason she had quit when her father retired. She had wanted no further contact with him even on a business level.

"You've met him—Jerry Phillips. We were introduced at the Montgomerys' party."

"He's a friend of Drew's, and if I'm thinking of the right guy, he's about five-eight, with black curly hair," Stacy said, pleased for the other girl.

"Yup. He works for one of the big oil companies," Katie explained.

"In this town you can hardly get away from oil, can you?" Stacy said drily.

"Nope." Katie smiled.

By the time they finished their meal, Stacy was feeling much better. Katie's genial companionship had acted like a soothing tonic.

When she returned home, Stacy put her package of books on a side table along with her purse and slumped down into the leather armchair, kicking off her shoes and letting them drop to the carpet with a muffled thump. Her eyelids drooped with fatigue, but as soon as she closed her eyes, unbidden, her mind conjured up visions of Drew. She sighed and for a moment gave herself up to the vicarious pleasure his image evoked.

She had heard that men could make love without being in love, but she had never understood how such an intimate act could ever be shared indiscriminately. She had let all the warmth of her bottled-up emotions come pouring forth, exulting in their release. And though Drew seemed to have reciprocated, she didn't have any experience on which to base a comparison, she mused ruefully. As far as she knew, he treated every woman in bed the same way. She winced at the stab of pain which seared through her.

Stacy continued to sit for several more minutes until the peal of the doorbell summoned her.

Assuming it was probably a salesperson, Stacy was startled when she swung open the door. Dorothy Pitman waited on the stoop.

"Dorothy! What a surprise!"

"Stacy . . . thank God you're home! I . . . I've driven straight in from Rockport."

Bewildered by her obvious agitation, Stacy quickly motioned her in.

"Dorothy, what's wrong?"

She took a deep breath, her hands clenched. "Drew's been hurt."

"No!" Stacy shook her head in disbelief.

"Yes, it's true . . . he's unconscious."

Pulling herself together, Stacy asked, 'Where is he?" *How ironic!* Stacy thought distractedly. *I don't even know where he is!*

"At the hospital in New Orleans."

"New Orleans," she repeated weakly.

"The man who called said he'd tried to get in touch with you, but when there wasn't any answer . . ."

"I've been out shopping all day," interjected Stacy.

"So he called me," Dorothy finished. "I've phoned for plane reservations. There's a flight leaving in an hour."

"Good." Stacy found her shoes and bent over to slip them on, saying, "If we leave immediately we should be able to make it."

"Pack a few things first, in case we have to stay." Dorothy suggested practically. "I'll lock up the house."

"Yes . . . good idea." Her words were spoken as Stacy dashed up the stairs. In less than ten mintues she returned with a bag containing not only clothing for herself, but also several items for Drew. She had recalled that one of her father's first requests when he was hospitalized was for his personal belongings.

Although Stacy felt a bit steadier, she was grateful

when Dorothy chose to drive to the airport. Once they were on their way, Dorothy tersely outlined the details of Drew's accident. He had been out on an offshore rig, and when it exploded he had gotten knocked against the superstructure. They had brought in a helicopter to lift him off, and it had been met by an ambulance which had taken him to the hospital.

Knowing that Dorothy had to concentrate on driving, Stacy remained silent after the other woman laid out the bare facts, caught up in her own depressing thoughts. She had no idea what they would face when they got to New Orleans. Head injuries could be so unpredictable.

They reached the airport in record time, with just minutes to spare. Stacy arranged for the car to be parked while Dorothy checked in and picked up the tickets. They were the last passengers to board the plane before the cabin door was sealed.

"Well . . . we made it," said Stacy, relieved.

"Just in time," Dorothy observed.

"I want to thank you for arranging everything." Stacy's eyes lingered on Dorothy. "I'm glad you're with me." She laid her hand across the woman's arm.

"I couldn't let my only son lie alone in some strange hospital."

"You really love him, don't you?" Stacy said softly.

"Is there any doubt?"

"Not as far as I'm concerned . . ."

"But you think Drew might not be so positive?" Dorothy questioned shrewdly.

"Yes." Stacy regarded Drew's mother closely, but she seemed to accept her answer without offense. Dorothy's eyes took on a distant look.

"I've always loved my son dearly, but when I lost my second baby and then my husband . . . I sort of withdrew into myself and allowed my painting to take over my life." She glanced at Stacy. "You see, I had no fear of it hurting me."

"I understand," Stacy murmured, patting the older woman's hand sympathetically.

"I just hope it's not too late. . . ." Dorothy's voice broke.

"Drew's going to be okay . . . I just know he is." Her words were sincere. Stacy refused to believe that Drew would die; they had come too far to have everything destroyed now!

Dorothy's eyes filled with compassion. "You love my son very much." It was a simple statement and Stacy nodded her head. "I'm very glad he's found a girl like you. Drew's very lucky."

"Thank you. . . . He's pretty special," responded Stacy.

"Yes, he is."

They did not speak much during the rest of the flight; both women were plagued by uncertainty, and Stacy kept glancing at her watch.

Although the flight was mercifully brief, the taxi journey to the hospital was exasperatingly slow. Rush-hour traffic blocked their progress, but when they arrived at the medical center they were greeted with good news. The doctor handling the case informed them that Drew had regained consciousness and had spoken lucidly with him. The after-effects of little rest (Stacy flushed; fortunately, no one seemed to notice) and of shock had resulted in his drifting off to sleep.

"Can we see him?" Stacy asked when the doctor finished.

He gave his consent and instructed a nurse to show them to Drew's room with the unnecessary order not to disturb his rest.

The nurse left them alone and they sat mutely waiting for Drew to awaken. Stacy noticed that except for a purple bruise near his hair line, he appeared quite unaffected. His breathing was natural and deep, his chest slowly rising and falling under its pristine covering. This was the only opportunity she had had to observe him asleep, and she was amazed at how peaceful he looked. His mouth was turned up in a half-smile and the muscles of his rugged features were relaxed; he seemed so vulnerable, like a small boy.

Time dragged and Stacy was becoming restless when over an hour later Drew's eyelids fluttered and opened. Stacy sprang from her chair and firmly grasped the large hand he held out to her. "Hello, sleepyhead."

Drew grinned sheepishly, staring into her eyes. "Hello, Stacy. Sorry to give you such a scare."

"That's all right. You're going to be okay. The doctor said the X rays showed no internal injuries." She paused. "I brought someone with me." She indicated the other side of the bed. "Your mother came, too."

Drew moved his head, his eyes widening in surprise. "Mama," he said, stretching out his other hand, and the older woman took it joyfully, her eyes swimming with tears.

"I'll be back in a moment." Gently, Stacy disentangled his fingers and went out into the hallway to wait. Dorothy's claim had precedence at this moment, and she was content to have it be so.

When Dorothy opened the heavy door, her jubilant expression told the whole story.

"Thank you, Stacy." Dorothy enfolded the younger woman in her arms and held her close. Then she released her, saying, "It's your turn now. I'll go get some coffee." She walked off down the corridor, her high heels ringing loud in the hospital's quiet.

With a deep breath Stacy pushed open the door and

then paused just inside. Drew looked much the same, but Stacy detected an air of suppressed excitement.

"Come, sit down." He patted the side of the bed, and she went over and perched on the high bed, her legs dangling, her hands propped on either side of him for balance.

"How are you feeling?" she asked when he seemed disinclined to say anymore.

"Pretty good . . . considering."

"You're lucky it wasn't more serious."

"The doctor said I'd a thick head."

"I knew that," she agreed with a touch of humor.

He cast her a wry glance. "I guess I deserved that—I've been quite dense about Mother's feelings."

"Yes. She really cares for you," Stacy affirmed.

"Well, we've finally got that cleared up."

"I'm glad."

"Are you?"

"Of course."

"Why?" He stared at her quizzically as she fumbled for an answer. Before she could respond, he went on: "You know us that well, hmm?"

Stacy could only nod her head. She discerned a strange gleam in his eyes.

"You haven't kissed your husband yet." Drew pulled her down to him.

"Oh, Drew," she murmured as she complied, tears sliding silently down her cheeks.

He tilted up her chin with one finger. "Weeping . . . for me?"

Straightening up, Stacy wiped her face with the back of her hand, sniffed audibly, and searched the nightstand for a tissue.

"Here . . . let me." His arms snaked around her back and he brought her back down to him, flicking away the tears with infinite sweetness. Then before she could move away he buried her face in the curve of his shoulder. "You're too good for me, my darling," he breathed in her ear.

Startled by his words of endearment, Stacy raised her head and stared. It was as though the sun had broken through the clouds; now she saw his eyes glow with devotion. She was no longer afraid of being rebuffed. "I love you, Drew," she said simply.

With a muffled groan he crushed her to him, passionately kissing her. Time was suspended.

Gently, Stacy eased away and contemplated his tortured expression. "What's wrong?"

"I can't say them, Stacy."

For over thirty years he had built a wall around his emotions, and she realized that they would need time to completely destroy the barrier. "They are there," Stacy told him, placing her palm over his chest. "In your heart, darling." This time she leaned down and pressed his mouth with hers, giving him proof of her love and acceptance.

As she released his lips she heard him say softly, "I love you."

She was overjoyed, but suddenly she realized that the words were not important. They were only one outward expression of all the emotions which they shared.

She smiled and said lightly, knowing it would embarrass this man to play it any other way, "That wasn't so hard, was it?"

"Nope. . . . Come here, you witch." He put a hand around her head and brought it down for a tantalizing kiss. "I've missed you," he said, letting her go for a moment. "You don't know how hard it's been to keep my hands off you."

Focusing on his face, she said with a twinkle, "So that's why you've been so abominable these past few weeks."

"Until last night . . ." His mouth curled upward at her pink color. "I hated to let you go on our wedding night, but I'd have hated myself more if I had taken you after you started crying."

"So you did remember!" she interjected.

"Sure. . . . I thought it would be better to start fresh and give you a chance to get to know me, uncomplicated by sex."

"I've been so foolish," she confessed. "I knew that you were physically attracted to me, but you've sounded so . . . so . . ." Her voice trailed off and she saw his expression change to one of amusement.

"From the beginning I knew you were the woman for me. I dreaded the thought of leaving you alone with all those oil men—especially with Paul Elmwood trying to lure you."

Stacy laughed, and he looked at her with mock reproof. "Paul's very lucky I didn't smash his face in when I caught the two of you in the garden."

Running a finger across his clenched jaw, Stacy said lightheartedly, "I never would have guessed."

"Don't get saucy with me, woman! You're in an extremely vulnerable position." He grinned at her devilishly. "These hospital gowns are indecent . . . they couldn't find any large enough."

"You wicked man! Your mother might be back at any minute."

"So what?" he said disdainfully, his normal arrogance resurging.

"So . . . I think I'll move." She tried to pull out of Drew's arms, but he pinned her against his chest.

"Oh, no, you don't." And with that he proceeded to thoroughly kiss her as though making up for lost time. Stacy did not struggle.

Neither of them noticed the door glide open or heard it close.

Several minutes later when the nurse came by to check on her patient's condition, Dorothy cornered her. Her voice was so penetrating that when the nurse continued into the room all she saw was Stacy standing at her husband's bedside holding his hand.

Drew flashed his wife a mischievous grin.